Cowboy Christmas: A Gay Erotic Tale

By

Phillip Cook

Chapter One

It was all my fault! I shouldn't fall in love so easily. That's a sure-fire way to get your heart broken in a hurry. My only excuse is that I'm young and don't have a lot of experience, or any experience at all. At eighteen years old I'm still a virgin and it appears I'm destined to remain one. For at least a little while longer anyway.

I trusted him. I shouldn't have. I thought he was my friend. He wasn't. So, it was all my fault I got tangled up with him in the first place.

Now I'm on my way to my uncle's dude ranch. Been on this bus for the last six hours. We should arrive shortly, and a driver is set to pick me up once I get there. I had to get away from my former life. Quit college, which didn't make my parents happy at all. They agreed to let me sort things out my own way only if I went down to the ranch and work for my uncle. They think it might teach me some responsibilities to work hard day in and day out. I was willing to do anything to get away from Barry.

My parents were surprised, to say the least, when I admitted this was all over a boy. They didn't have a clue I was gay. Most likely because I never dated or brought anyone home. I was a shy kid who didn't have many friends. So, my parents went on the assumption the reason I didn't have any girlfriends was simply because I was a big fat loser.

Which isn't far from the truth considering what transpired between Barry and me.

As I sat on the bus watching the scenery of fields and barns passing me by, I tried to put the past out of my head. What Barry said. What he did to me. I knew I had to shake thoughts of him out of my mind for good. It was no use to keep playing the events in my head on a loop.

My eyes were getting heavy and needed rest so thought I would close them for a while. Soon, I drifted off to sleep and had a dream of a monster chasing me down an empty dark street. With no one around to save me the monster had me cornered.

I woke with a start to the booming voice of the bus driver announcing my stop. Sweat covered my forehead and my heart pumped heavily in my chest.

Looking out my window, I saw a dusty little town somewhere in West Texas.

My final destination still an hour away. Since buses don't run up there, the driver my uncle sent will take me the rest of the way. I didn't get a lot of sleep, so I'm still tired and groggy from the short nap.

I dragged myself off the bus and collected my luggage, which were two small suitcases, and searched for the car picking me up.

There were three taxis, a couple of fancy cars which looked like expensive sport cars, and an old beat up rusted red Ford pick-up truck. A tall cowboy stood in front holding up a sign which read "Phillip."

It looked as though my uncle had gone all out for me. Not that I expected much, but I did wonder why my uncle couldn't have picked me up himself. It had been ages since I had seen him.

I nervously approached the cowboy. He was sexy as hell and my heart started beating a mile a minute the closer I got and I could swear my cock grew three sizes its normal size. He had a couple days' growth of whiskers on his face and a strong square jaw. His eyes were an ocean blue and dark eyebrows made them look deep and sexy. His cowboy hat covered his short, dark hair. He stood well over six feet and wore a faded jean jacket and faded blue jeans, a plaid blue shirt was under his jacket, and a big belt buckle with the state of Texas imprinted on it adorned his belt. Old dirty Cowboy boots completed his look.

I could tell by the tight jeans his package was huge.

I admonished myself for looking, but in my defense, it was just too obvious to ignore.

He appeared to be older than me by at least ten years, making him roughly twenty-eight. He was a manly man. Fit and rugged. He smelled of sandalwood and a musky male scent that made my heart want to leap out of my chest and do somersaults.

I had to try not to think of him in a sexual way. I made that mistake with Barry and it blew up in my face like an exploding tomato. I fall in love too easily and this time, I told myself, to stop before I act. This cowboy most likely was straight and would never be interested in me. Even if he were gay, I doubted I would be his type.

"You Phillip?" He asked me in a deep sexy voice giving me tingles in my nether regions. I nodded my head yes, losing my own voice temporarily. "I was expecting someone older. You still in high school?"

My face flushed red. *He thinks I'm a kid,* I thought. *Well, I suppose to him, I seemed like one. After all, I finished high school not more than six months before.*

"N-no. I just turned eighteen and I'm a freshman in college." I informed him.

"Gosh. You look like you're fifteen," he tipped his hat back and placed his hands on his hips, scrutinizing me. "My bad," he smiled.

I wasn't sure if I should be mad at him, so I just shrugged. He tossed the sign in the back of the truck and took both my suitcases, throwing them back there too.

"Will they be okay back there?" I asked.

"They won't likely blow away. It's not like this old pick-up goes all that fast," he said, winking at me. "Hop in, your uncle is expecting us and I'm a might hungry and thought we'd get something to eat on the way back to the ranch."

I opened the door to find a lot of trash from fast food places in the passenger's seat.

"Oh, sorry 'bout that. I eat on the run a lot. Just push it all on the floor."

"Um...okay." I hesitated a moment, wondering if the trash might contain bacteria or something. Deciding I couldn't stand there all day looking like a dork, I pushed the trash to the floor and climbed in on the cleared spot.

"There now, that wasn't so bad was it?" He chuckled, "it looked there for a minute you thought them wrappers were going to bite you."

"Sorry," was all I said as I closed the creaky door.

"That's alright, Phillip. You'll get used to the way things are around here in no time, I'm sure. Oh, where are my manners. Didn't introduce myself. Rick Mason." He shot out a hand for me to shake. I took it gently and he grasped my hand firmly and shook a couple of times making my arm feel like it was made of Jell-O. I reclaimed my hand and discreetly rubbed it. He had a powerful handshake. "Hey, better shut the door properly," he reached over me, his underarm right in my nose as he reopened the passenger's side door and then slammed it shut. His odor was intoxicating. He sat back on his side of the seat and smiled sheepishly. "You have to slam the door of this thing, otherwise it will fly open. We don't want to lose you, now do we? Your uncle would kill me."

"My uncle made you pick me up?" I asked as I buckled myself into the death trap.

"Actually, I volunteered. It got me out of mending fences," he smiled, showing all his sparkling white teeth. He was the sexiest man I had ever laid eyes upon. And that included Barry.

"You think I would have to mend fences?" I wondered out loud.

"I'm sure your Uncle Hank and Clem will find something for you to do." Clem was my uncle's lover of thirty years. "After all, idle hands are the devil's workshop, as they say. Or is it playthings? I get it confused sometimes." Rick said. He started up the truck. It wouldn't go at first and he had to try and restart it a couple of times before the engine roared to life. "Let's get something to eat. Need to get some gas too. The gas station is across the street from the diner. One stone, two birds," he said holding up first one then two fingers as if demonstrating his point.

We drove in silence for a few minutes while I took furtive glances at him and his handsome features. He was truly a rugged cowboy with all the fixings. My dick stirred in my jeans and I was afraid I would get a boner and that he would notice. I wondered what he would say or do if he knew I had the hots for him. I thought back to Barry; of just a few short weeks ago and what transpired between us, and what he did.

Would Rick do the same? Would he be as cruel as Barry? He worked for my uncle, an openly gay rancher who's been living with his lover for the past 30 years. You would think he would be okay with me being gay too and having the hots for him.

Would he be more flattered than Barry? I wondered.

I put these thoughts aside, thinking it was of no use? He would never be interested in me. Gay or straight, I just wasn't the kind of guy someone would fall in love with so easily.

"Quiet, ain't ya," Rick broke the silence.

"Sorry, just a lot on my mind," I said, softly.

"Don't be sorry. Quiet is good sometimes. Just that I'm used to talking and getting to know someone."

Does he really want to get to know me? I mused.

"There's nothing much to know about me," I said.

"I bet that ain't true. Everybody's got a story," we were quiet again for a few minutes. He looked as if he was thinking of something, like he was trying to figure out my story. "I bet it has something to do with a girl," he hit his hands on the steering wheel and smiled excitedly like he had just figured out the meaning of life. "There's always a girl."

He was far off the mark.

"No. I never had any girl problems."

He frowned.

"Never?" He looked askance at me. "Never is a long time. How old did you say you were? Eighteen?" I nodded. "Boy howdy, and never had any girl problems, ever?"

"It's because I never had a girlfriend," I suddenly admitted, and regretted it soon after.

My stomach felt queasy.

"Find that hard to believe. A cute guy like you."

Wait! Did he just say I was cute?

"I'm not cute," I said in a low voice. "And I'm not interested in girls."

"Hold the horses!" He yelled and I nearly jumped a foot out of my seat hitting my head on the truck's ceiling. "You're gay?"

"Um...I guess," I rubbed my head. I didn't really know what to say. Was he mad, delighted, surprised? I couldn't read his emotions very well.

"Well, I'll be dogged!" He had some strange expressions. "Your uncle is gay too."

"Yeah, I know," I said quietly.

"I never knew it could run in families."

"Well, it does. Sometimes, I guess."

"Well, I'll be a stud that just got fucked by a steer! That's amazing!" I was trying to figure out what his last expression meant, when he said: "Then it must be boy troubles."

I took a deep breath.

"Sort of. But I'd rather not talk about it."

"Sure enough. I understand that. But if you need someone to talk to, I'm around. Remember that."

"Yes sir," I said.

"Sir?" He laughed. "I'm barely ten years older than you. Call me Rick."

"Alright, Rick," I smiled, relaxing a little.

"You know, there's one thing I noticed about you."

"What's that?" I asked, perplexed.

"You sure do talk proper. Ain't you ever said ain't?"

"No."

"Even when you were a kid?" He looked at me as we had stopped at a red light, expecting an answer to his query.

"No. My mom would have had a fit."

"Well. You are bound to say ain't after hangin' with me for a spell. I tend to rub off on people," he winked at me.

With my face burning as hot as coals in a fire, I was sure my face blushed bright red.

***

About half an hour later, we pulled into a gas station and a young guy about my age with dark blond hair wearing torn jeans and a gray shirt came bounding over to us with a bright smile and a twinkle in his eyes. He seemed especially excited to see Rick.

"Howdy, Rick. Fill her up?"

"Yup, Sam. Fill her all the way up and if you could wash the windshield too, would be mighty grateful."

"Sure thing," Sam said and went to filling up the truck with gas then grabbed a rag and a spray bottle of cleaning solution and began spraying the dirty windshield.

"Full service?" I whispered.

"Yup. Sam here can be mighty obliging."

My stomach began to rumble as we stepped out of the truck and I realized I hadn't eaten anything for hours, not since leaving Dallas.

"Hey, Phillip," Rick called over to me. "Would you order me a cheeseburger and fries and a chocolate shake? I need to take a leak."

"Um...sure," I said.

"Thanks." I saw him walking towards the back of the gas station and watched his sexy ass in his tight cowboy jeans. *'Boy, what I wouldn't give,'* I thought.

The diner stood across the street, an older wood framed building in need of a paint job, with a sign standing in the small parking lot which said, Winnie's. The street between the gas station and the diner was a narrow road with barely any cars driving on it, just one or two, so it took no time to walk across.

"Hi, have a seat. I'll be with her in a minute, hon," a middle-aged waitress, with red hair pulled up into a bun, and a blue uniform with a white frilly apron, said as I walked in.

I sat in a booth near the window which faced the gas station, and gazed out across the road, watching the gas attendant, Sam, as he finished up with the truck. He looked around as if searching for prying eyes, and then headed towards the back of the building, the same direction Rick disappeared behind.

"What will it be?" The waitress was poised to take my order with pad and pencil at the ready.

"Two cheeseburgers, two orders of fries, and two chocolate shakes," I said.

"You plan on eating all that yourself or are you expecting company?" By the smile on her face I could tell she was teasing.

"I'm expecting Rick," I said. For some reason, I thought maybe she would know who I meant by just the first name.

"Oh Rick. Hey, you must be Hank's nephew." She must have seen the shocked expression on my face. "It's a small town, honey. Word gets around quick. I'll be back with your order in a jiff," she said, putting the pencil behind her ear.

"Thanks. Um...where's the restroom by the way?" I thought I would take my own leak while waiting for the food.

"Sorry, it's out of order. But you can use the gas station's," she informed me, pointing the way.

"Thanks. I'll be right back."

I went back out over to the gas station and meandered towards the back looking for the restroom. I wasn't sure if Rick would still be in there and if I would have to wait.

When I got to the men's room, I saw the door slightly ajar. Most gas stations that I knew kept their restrooms locked. It creeped me out a little. I wondered where Rick went or if there was another restroom he was using. I didn't have time to think about it as I was bursting to go and starting to do a little dance. I rushed inside the restroom and closed the door. A minute later I was done with my business, much to the relief of my bladder.

I thought Rick must surely be back at the diner by now and headed in that direction when I heard moaning coming from the back of the gas station. Being the curious sort, I decided to take a quick peep.

What I saw shocked the socks off me.

Both Rick and Sam were naked. Well, Rick still had his Cowboy hat and boots on. Rick was behind Sam and had him bent over plowing into his ass. Sam had a look of pure pleasure on his face.

"Oh, yeah! Fuck me cowboy! Fuck me hard!" Sam kept repeating over and over.

"Sammy, you're so tight! When was the last time you got fucked?"

"Since the last time you fucked me, about a week ago."

"Oh God! This feels great. I'm about to cum!"

Rick pulled out of Sam's ass. Sam knelt before him taking off the condom and throwing it aside then wrapped his lips around Rick's huge dickhead and jacked the base, milking him of his juices.

"Oh God! Oh God!" Rick shouted. Cum dribbled out from the corners of Sam's mouth and some onto his hand. Rick slumped down on a pile of tires. It was the first time I really saw his dick. It was a beautiful sight. It looked at least nine inches, cut. He had a nice set of balls too.

I thought about leaving when Rick got up and pulled Sam up from his knees by his underarms, turned him around, facing my hiding spot, and pulled Sam close to his naked body. He caressed Sam's chest and down to his flat stomach, through his thick blond pubes to his hard dick. Rick took hold of Sam's dick with an iron grip and slid his fist up and down his swollen member.

Sam moaned and shook. His dickhead leaked pre-cum, which no doubt made it easier for Rick to jack it with those rough callused hands of his. Rick gained speed and went faster and faster as Sam thrashed against his naked flesh.

"Oh God, Rick! I'm gonna cum!" Sam shot four powerful loads out of his dick, splattering the cement ground they were on, and covering Rick's jacking hand. Sam slouched back against Rick who loosened his grip on Sam's softening dick. With labored breaths, they each slowly calmed down from their climaxes braced against each other. Rick leaned in and kissed Sam on the lips.

I thought it best to leave the two lovebirds alone and went back to the diner. More morose than when I had arrived several minutes earlier. I wondered why all the good men were taken. I slouched in the booth, arms crossed, and listened to the radio playing Let It Snow.

Chapter Two

'Silver bells, silver bells. It's Christmas time in the city,' the radio in the old faded red pick-up truck blared out with a country twang. "Ring-a-ling, hear them sing. Soon it will be Christmas day," Rick joined in singing with a nice baritone voice. I sat quietly beside him, pondering over what I saw behind the gas station. Rick fucking that Sam guy senseless. I glanced over at him all dressed in his jeans and jacket once more, his window open and his hair fluttering in the wind, but somehow, I kept remembering how he looked naked except for his boots and hat.

He caught me ogling him as he turned his head my way. I blushed and averted my eyes, starring out the window.

Lunch had been good. I managed to act as though nothing had happened when Rick strode into the diner. He had a big grin plastered on his handsome face. He seemed to be satisfied and had a much-needed release of some sort. Of course, I knew the reason why, though he didn't know I knew, and I had to pretend I didn't know.

The waitress delivered our food as he entered. She smiled at Rick and me, then headed back into the kitchen.

"The food looks good," I said, my voice sounding a little squeaky.

"Best burgers in Texas," he said as he took a bite like a ravenous animal. "Sorry I took so long, but I guess I really had to go," he said. Rick held his hamburger with both hands, it was a pretty big burger, and took another giant bite out of it and began chewing and rolling his eyes in the back of his head like he was having another orgasm. "Like I said, best burger on earth."

"You said Texas," I reminded him.

He rolled his eyes.

"Well, if you're going to nitpick. Go on, eat up. You'll see what I'm talking about."

I took a small bite out of mine and had to agree. It was the best I ever had. Though, I wasn't really all that hungry anymore and wasn't sure I would be able to eat the whole thing, but I did eat half of it.

"We're gonna have to do something about your appetite," Rick said, as he drew the last fry into his mouth. "You're gonna learn to eat the whole thing in one gobble when we're through with you. What with all the work out at the ranch, you're gonna have to have a big ole appetite."

My mind flashed back to the gas station and Rick fucking Sam. I was beginning to get a big appetite alright and it wasn't for food. But I was sure Rick would never be interested in me. He was a hot cowboy and I was basically a nerdy city boy.

"You alright?" Rick asked pulling me out of my reverie and back into the present, in the truck. He had turned down the radio where I barely heard the Christmas song playing. "You looked like you were a million miles away."

"I'm fine," I answered him, though not sure if it was a truthful answer. "Just thinking."

"Well, that's alright. You probably have a lot on your mind. What with you coming down here to work on your uncle's ranch and not knowing what to expect and all."

We drove in silence for a few minutes. Some of the surroundings were beginning to look familiar to me from when I used to visit when I was a kid. The old general store still stood where it had been for decades. It's an old wood framed building with an old-fashioned Coca Cola sign, advertising the refreshing drink. And the old barber shop next door where my uncle used to take me to get my hair cut while he played checkers with one of the other ranchers in the area. I hadn't been here in ten years, about the time my parents found out my uncle was gay. I guess they thought he would be a bad influence on me, but he had been nothing but kind to me. A second father who took care of me when I came to visit on hot summer days.

Now that my parents knew I was gay, they figured my uncle was the best person to be around as a role model. They had slowly accepted my uncle's sexuality over the years and when they found out about me, they reached out to him to seek help in navigating my so-called life. He was more than happy to help.

I glimpsed the old movie theater my uncle took me too when I was eight. We had some good times watching some good old movies in that place and eating popcorn and drinking soda.

"Do you and Sam ever go to movies in that theater?" I asked as I pointed out the window at the Old Majestic. "They used to show some good old ones that was made a long time ago there. Like from the 40's, 50's, 60's, and 70's."

Rick stared at me; his demeanor seemed as if he was thinking of something. His handsome face had a quizzical visage.

"What made you ask about Sam and me?" He inquired.

"Well, um...," I wasn't sure what to say. "Well, you see, when I was waiting in the diner I had to use the restroom and it was out of order so the waitress said I could use the one at the gas station. So, I thought I would have to wait for you, but you weren't there. When I finished I heard noises in the back and went to check, and saw you and Sam...," I muttered all that rather quickly, I wasn't sure if he understood what I said.

"Ah, you saw Sam and me doing the nasty," he nodded his head in understanding and grinning. At least he didn't seem mad. "Well, Sam's not my boyfriend. He's a fuck buddy and we don't really hang out much anywhere. Actually, we only do it at the gas station. He has this thing for public sex and the thrill we might get caught really turns him on. And I guess, this time, we did get caught. Only we didn't know it." He laughed at that and shook his head in amazement. He looked back at me slyly and smirked. "So, did you pull your pants down and jerk your dick?"

"No!" I blushed, turning away from his steely gaze.

"It's alright if you did. I'm sure it must have been hot to watch."

"You're not mad? That I watched you two...you know."

We pulled up at a stop sign. No cars were around, yet we lingered there.

"Fuck. The word is fuck. No. I ain't mad. Hell, if it had been me catching you and Sam, I would have jerked my cock. Hell, who am I kidding," he threw his hands up in the air, shaking his head, "I would have joined in." He winked at me as he laid his hands back on the steering wheel. He had a way of making me blush. "Why didn't you?" He asked after a moment of silence.

"What?" My heart palpitated and every part of my body felt on fire with his words. I had a sudden yearning to be touched by those rough hands. To be caressed and fondled. To be loved in a way Barry could never give me. To yield to his soft kisses and his strong embrace.

"Join in. I think Sam would have liked that."

Forget Sam, I thought. *I just want you. I want to be your boyfriend and love you forever.*

I shook the thought out of my head almost as soon as it had appeared. I fall in love too easily, and Rick wasn't offering me love. He wasn't even offering me sex. He had said Sam would have liked me to join them, Rick might have begrudgingly agreed, if only to please his lover...er.... fuck buddy.

"Would you have?" I asked, quietly, wanting to know, yet dreading the answer.

"Yup. Might have been a lot of fun. Hell," instead of going straight, in the direction of the ranch, he turned off onto a dirt road, "we can still have some fun."

"This isn't the way to the ranch. Is it?" I said dumbly. The words he had just said not registering.

"Nope. Just thought you and me can have some fun. Like me and Sam did."

I gulped. I couldn't believe what he was suggesting.

"Are you serious?" I asked, barely above a whisper.

"Yup," he said simply as he drove the truck behind some trees and pulled into a stop. "This is a pretty private and secluded road. We aren't likely to get interrupted here."

My heart pounded and my cock throbbed. *Was I really going to have sex with this hot cowboy?* My whole body shook with the thought.

"I'm a virgin," I blurted, my hands quickly covered my mouth.

He stared at me for a moment as if to ponder his next move.

"We don't have to fuck. There are lots of things we can do to ease you into man on man sex."

He shut the motor off and undid his belt, unbuckled his pants, slid his jeans down revealing black boxer briefs, and slid those down next, just enough to show his black pubic hair and the base of his dick, He took my hand and placed it on his bush.

"Feel me," he breathed. It wasn't an order. It sounded more like a plea.

I shivered even though it was probably eighty degrees. This was really happening. This hot cowboy wanted to do something sexy with me. I have never had an opportunity like this. I was scared yet exhilarated by this situation. I took a deep breath and allowed my fingers to touch his private area. Feeling his pubic hair, it surprised me by how soft it felt, almost like silk. I ran my fingers through the hairs and reached the base of his dick which was still hidden under the fabric of his briefs, though I could see the huge bulge. His dick seemed to come to life as my fingers slowly made their way down its length. He grabbed my hand and pushed it further down on his cock until I reached the head. The tip of his dick spongy and sticky and warm. Now my whole hand was inside his briefs and my fingers gently grasped around his thick cock. It pulsed and hardened with my touch.

He quickly pulled my hand out and pulled up his jeans. Was it over? I felt shattered. I was sure I did something wrong. Or maybe it was a joke.

"I'll be right back," he said urgently.

He got out and went to the back of the truck. I couldn't see what he was doing but several seconds later he was at my door opening it and ushering me out.

"Let's do it in the back of the truck. More room."

He led me around to the bed of his truck. He had lowered the gate and placed a large towel down. My suitcases were stacked neatly at the very back.

"Sex can get messy and I would rather not explain splattered cum on the truck if I can help it," he said sheepishly. "Now, in order for us to do this, you need to take off all your clothes." He took his jacket off and unbuttoned his shirt. "Oh, better take this off," he took off his hat. "Sam wanted me to leave it on while we fucked, but for what we're gonna do it would be a whole lot easier to leave it off. But I can leave my boots on if you want."

"Sure," I said, noncommittally.

I think I was in shock, and still shivered from the possibility of his touch.

I had removed my shirt and felt embarrassed by how skinny I was compared to this hunky cowboy. I was hesitant to get undressed because I had body issues. I was too thin, too pale, and too smooth. I had pubic hair, which was the same color as my brown hair, but everywhere else was pretty much smooth.

"Hurry up. We need to get back to the ranch before they send a posse looking for us," he said as he slipped off his underwear.

By the time I got down to my briefs, he had already shed all he clothes and sat on the gate of his truck completely naked while pulling his boots back on. He got off his truck and stood before me in all his glory. His nine-inch dick thrust out from his body and his juicy balls hung low. He was gorgeous. I wanted to pinch myself to check if this was really happening. However, I was afraid I would wake up and the sight before me now would fade away forever.

"Wow, you have a nice little body," he said, and I blushed yet again.

"No, I don't," I said, staring at the ground, kicking at some pebbles. "You do though," I said in a whisper.

"No. Really. You have a nice body. Now get up on the truck." He stuck his hand out and I grabbed hold of it. He gently pulled me forward and helped me onto the truck. He took a quick feel of my balls and dick and I got tingly all over. "Don't worry. This will be fun," he assured me. "Lie down on the towel." I did as I was told. His beautiful body above me, his strong muscled legs on either side of my quaking body. He lowered himself down and laid himself on my smaller frame. His face mere inches from mine and his dick pressing down against my own. He brought his mouth towards my lips and gently kissed me. He looked down at me and caressed my cheek. "You're like a porcelain doll. You look so fragile."

"I'm not as fragile as I look," I told him. I was afraid he would change his mind and not do anything with me. As scared as I was, I wanted him.

"I just mean that you're more beautiful than you know."

I knew I wasn't beautiful, or handsome, or even cute. I was just me. But it made me feel special to hear him say it.

His dick smashed with mine as he kissed my lips once more. He moved down to my chin, then neck, he slowly slithered down my body placing kisses as he went. Licking and nibbling as my hot flesh burned with desire.

He reached my dick and wrapped his hand around it. I moaned and writhed. No one had ever touched my dick before, and the feeling overwhelmed me. He looked me in the eye and stuck out his tongue. Almost too painfully slow, he reached out towards my dickhead and finally made contact with the tip of his tongue to my piss slit. He swirled his tongue around the rim of my dickhead and licked down the length to the base and to my balls. He sucked on my balls, putting them in his mouth and washing them with his saliva. He licked back up to the tip of my dick and opened his mouth wide and my dick disappeared into his mouth as he closed his luscious lips tight around my shaft. He went all the way down until his nose pressed against my pubes and then made the journey back up again.

My legs were shaking, and my dick was aching. My face contorted in uncontrollable expressions of sexual lust. He had awakened something within me. Something that was dying to get out, my sexuality and hidden desires. Lust filled my being, my body flushed with the heat pulsating from his sucking mouth.

He repeated the process with my dick a few more times. Up and down. From head to base. His tongue lapping at my juices which were flowing freely as he sucked my dick up in his warm, wet, and tender mouth. The incredible suction had my toes curling He kept sucking like some kind of vacuum hitting on my nerve endings.

He lifted off of my dick and looked into my eyes, his were filled with lust and want.

"Do you think you could do that? To me?" He asked, almost shyly, almost as if he thought I would say no.

I laid there on the towel in the back of his truck, trying to catch my breath. What he did to me felt amazing and I wanted to return the favor, so I nodded my head yes. He smiled and inverted his body over mine. His face in my crotch and his crotch in my face.

"We can do a sixty-nine so we can suck each other at the same time," he explained. His sexy cock was at my mouth and I tentatively took a quick lick and then another. His balls were hanging over my forehead. I opened my mouth and his dickhead slipped in. He pushed a little more in but not too much as if afraid of choking me. In the meantime, he went back to work on my dick. His lips were once again wrapped tightly around my dick, and he sucked and slobbered on it, driving me wild.

He played with my balls as he sucked on my cock, rolling my balls in his hand, His other hand kept busy jacking the base of my six inch cut dick, while he sucked on the head and first couple of inches. I reached up and played with his balls as he plunged his dick in and out of my mouth. He essentially fucked my mouth.

The taste of his dick was bitter yet sweet, the scent musky with the sweat of a hard day's work.

His fingers went lower, behind my balls, finding my hole. He played around with it, tapping it some, but not entering it. His dick slipped out of my hungry mouth, so I took the opportunity to go after his balls. I sucked them in and began chewing on them and rolling them around. He moaned around my dick, so I knew he really liked what I was doing to him.

He sucked me faster and harder. It was getting late and my uncle would be wondering what was taking us so long. Yet, I never wanted this to end but end it must.

I bucked my hips and he took all of me inside. My dick vibrated and salivated inside Rick's hot, moist mouth. He had me thrashing underneath him like a man being electrocuted.

"Oh God! Oh God! Oh God!" I chanted. He was going at my dick like a hungry animal, starved for the juices which flowed out of my dick and down his throat. "I'm gonna cum!" I practically screamed the warning. He paid no heed and kept sucking hard and furious. The first shot came suddenly, as he jacked my dick and his mouth remained around the head. After another two shots he stopped jacking and swallowed my dick whole. It remained buried inside his mouth as I shot out the rest of my load. "Oh God! Oh wow!" I shouted. "Ooh! Oh wow!" He moved back up to the head and squeezed out the final drops of cum onto his tongue. My body convulsed and shivered. I slumped back on the towel and rubbed my forehead, feeling dizzy and drained. My cock softened inside his mouth, it slipped out, greasy with cum and his saliva. I was spent and exhausted.

"How did you like you're first blow job?" He asked, squatting over my prone body, his hard dick, wet with my saliva, bobbed between his legs.

"Wow. It was really...wow. Better than I ever dreamed." I looked up and saw his still hard dick. I didn't finish him off yet. "I need to get back to sucking you," I said as I sat up.

"You don't have to. I can just jerk it."

"No. I want to," I assured him.

"Okay. But we have to hurry. I'll warn you when I'm about to cum."

He laid back and spread his long legs. I licked up his cock and took the head into my mouth. I wasn't an experienced cocksucker by any means, this was my first time, and first cock, after all, but I did my best to pleasure him using many of the techniques he had used on me. I had him moaning and writhing within seconds. To hurry the process, I jacked the bottom half of his dick while sucking the top half. I sucked hard and fast and my hand slid up and down in quick jacking motions on his slick pole. He was shaking and panting, and I thought he was getting close.

"Oh God, Phillip! Gonna Cum! Gonna fucking cum!" he yelled. I pulled off his dick because I wasn't sure if I was ready to swallow his load. I continued jacking him fast, and soon white cum spurted from his dick and shot straight up and came back down again on his stomach and on the towel. It was like it was raining cum, making quite a mess as he shot load after load, covering my hand, and splattering everywhere. "Oh wow!" he said as he slouched back on the towel, his dick spitting out the last little dribble of cum. "You were pretty good for a beginner," he smiled.

I beamed at the compliment. All I wanted to do was please him as he had pleased me.

"We better get dressed and get going," he said. "It's getting late."

As much as I would have liked to cuddle up with him for a while, I knew he was right. My uncle was expecting us.

***

We drove in silence the rest of the way. It was only another couple of miles or so to the ranch from where we had sex. He turned up the radio once more and listened to Santa Claus Is Coming to Town.

Christmas was in the air as we pulled into the ranch. Decorations all around: a manger scene, snowmen, Santa Claus, reindeer, Christmas lights all around. It might have been a winter wonderland, except there would be no snow.

My uncle greeted us as I stepped out of the truck with a huge smile on his aged face. He looked the same from when I saw him last, but just a little bit older with a gray beard and thinning white hair.

"Howdy Phillip," he came over and gave me a bear hug practically lifting me off the ground. "I see you finally made it." He turned to Rick. "What took y'all so long? We were expecting you over an hour ago."

"We decided to take the scenic route," Rick winked at me, grabbing my bags out of the truck.

"Well, that's okay, I suppose," my uncle said, scratching his head as if he was trying to remember something. "Oh, I almost forgot. We

20

have a new hire, Rick. He actually worked here before. I think you might remember him. He came back to town and needed a job."

An extremely handsome cowboy with blond wavy hair, which shone like spun gold in the afternoon sun, came walking up to us. He was quite muscular and wore tight faded blue jeans and a green plaid shirt that showed off his physique and the contours of his hard body. His cowboy boots were pulled up over the legs of his jeans and he looked about the same age as Rick.

He carried his white cowboy hat in his hand and waved it trying to get Rick's attention as he came towards us. He had a huge shit eating grin on his gorgeous face.

"Hi Rick," the cowboy said.

Rick dropped my bags and stared at the cowboy in wide eyed wonder.

"Luke! Oh my God." He rushed into Luke's arms and they embraced.

"Who's he?" I asked my uncle.

"Rick's ex," he said. "Looks like they might rekindle things though."

I couldn't believe my eyes as the lips which had been moments ago wrapped around my cock, now kissed this handsome cowboy.

Chapter Three

"It's been a hell of a long time, Luke," Rick said, holding onto Luke's arms in a tight grip and looking him squarely in the eyes as if trying to convey something meaningful. "Last I heard you were heading to Oklahoma."

"I did. I spent the last three years there working on a ranch. But I missed Texas. I missed you, Rick," it sounded as if he was choking back tears.

"Hell, I missed you too," Rick pulled Luke into another hug.

Feeling suddenly out of place and awkward, I just wanted to go to my room and settle in. I was beginning to fall for Rick, even though I just met the man, and knew I shouldn't be falling for someone who was bound to break my heart in a big way.

Rick was the total package: Extremely handsome, sexy, tall, well built, a huge dick, and he was a genuinely nice guy. He was a man's man. If he hadn't sucked my dick on the back of his truck, I would have thought he was straight. He was my first sexual experience and I had flutters in my stomach when I even thought of him. It's obvious he doesn't feel the same about me the way he's hanging all over his ex.

"Well, I think I'm going to unpack," I told my uncle. "You think it will be alright if I freshened up and take a nap before supper, been a long trip."

"Of course. We're having your favorite tonight. Meatloaf, mashed potatoes, and apple pie with homemade ice cream for dessert."

"Yum," I said. "Can't wait."

I went to retrieve my suitcases where Rick had abandoned them.

"Here, let me get those," Rick said. Breaking himself away from Luke at last.

"No, it's alright. I got them," I assured him. "Thanks for picking me up...and everything."

"It was my pleasure, Phillip," he winked.

"Let me go with you, Phillip. I want to show you the tree," Uncle Hank said. "Erika is dying to see you all grown up."

"Looking forward to seeing her too. I bet she did her own growing. You already got the tree?" I stopped and stared at my uncle in disbelief. He usually never put up a tree until a week before Christmas.

"Yup. An eight-footer spruce pine. We're going to decorate it after supper and have hot cocoa and sing Christmas carols. It's a tradition here at the ranch, well, a fairly new tradition. You'll soon see a lot of new things here at the ranch."

"Sounds like fun. I'm looking forward to it," I told him and meant it.

My uncle wasn't kidding. The tree was huge. You could smell the pine fill the room with its woodsy scent reminding us Christmas was near. The living room had a ten-foot ceiling so the Christmas star would fit perfectly with some space to spare. Being the youngest, the job always fell to me to place the star atop the tree. My dad would put me on his shoulders, and I reached for the top bough and proudly placed the star upon it. Sometimes I missed being a little kid and the magic Christmas seemed to be back then.

"Wow. That looks amazing," I said in awe. "It smells really good too."

"Yup. Rick sure knows how to pick 'em."

"Rick picked it?"

"Yup. He knows what kinds of trees we like around here, and I told him it had to be extra special for your Christmas with us."

"Well, thanks. It really is special," I put my luggage down and gave him an affectionate hug. "Uncle?"

"Yes nephew?" He always called me nephew when I call him Uncle.

"Is everyone around here gay?"

I could feel him smile.

"Not everyone. Jake is straight as far as I know."

"Jake?"

"Yeah. You'll meet him at supper. He's out fixing a fence on the north side of the ranch. He just broke up with his girlfriend a few weeks ago though, so if he gets horny enough, you'll never know what might happen," he laughed.

"Uncle!" I exclaimed, pulling back from the hug to give my uncle a scolding stare.

"Hey, there are a lot of guys around here that would love to swing on his big black cock."

"Uncle!" I said once more, aghast yet amused at his candidness. He didn't say things like that when I was a kid. Of course, I was a kid so he would have watched what he said around me.

"What nephew? It's only sex." He laughed his haughty laugh once again at the expression on my face. "Well, I suggest you rest up before supper. You must be dead tired."

"I am. Thanks. You putting me up in my old room?"

"Yup. Wouldn't have it any other way. Supper will be 6:30."

"Hi stranger," a young woman with long dark hair tied in a ponytail walked into the room.

"Erika?" I asked, astonished. She certainly had grown up from the little freckled faced girl I knew as a kid.

"Who else? Maybe you were expecting Santa Claus?" She laughed and gave me a hug. "It's good to see you, Pip."

She had given me that nick name when we were kids and I always hated it. I haven't heard it in years, suddenly realizing I don't hate it as much.

"Come on," she grabbed hold one of my suitcases, "I'll show you to your room."

"I think I can remember the way," I said.

"Well, I'll show you anyway, we have loads to talk about. It's been a little over ten years, after all. When we were eight or nine?"

I picked up the other suitcase.

"Well, lead the way."

When we entered my old room, I realized nothing much had changed, except maybe the sheets. They were once SpongeBob SquarePants, now they're a solid light blue with darker blue curtains hanging from the window. Everything else looked as if time had stood still. Same bed with iron headboard, same little desk and chair. Same window seat I used to sit on and stare out at the night sky when I was supposed to be asleep, that was my dreaming spot, I called it.

I never had any personal posters or pictures since I only stayed for the summers when I was six until I was eight, and one memorable Christmas when I was seven. The only thing that made it a kid's room were the sheets and curtains of a cartoon sponge.

After putting my suitcase on the floor, Erika sat on the bed with her legs dangling over the edge. Curiosity streaked her pretty face as if she had tons of questions for me. I began to unpack the few things I brought with me, feeling her eyes on me the whole time. It made me subconsciously squirm.

"So," she finally said, "do you have a boyfriend?"

I dropped the hanger I had just put a pair of jeans on and stood frozen, disbelief written all over my face.

"Relax," she said, chuckling in delight at my perplexity. "There are more gay dudes around here than straight. At least it seems that way. I tell myself that's the reason I can't get a date to the Christmas dance."

"But how did you..."

"Is it supposed to be a secret? I knew you were gay since you were eight."

"Really?" I found that hard to believe."

"Come on," she patted the bed, "let's sit and talk a while. You can finish unpacking later."

I sat beside her and she bumped my shoulder with hers giving me a sly look. "So, do you have a boyfriend?"

"No. What did my uncle tell you?"

"Oh, nothing," she shrugged her shoulders. "I just heard him and Clem talking."

"Eavesdropper," I accused.

"Get real. I can't help it if I overhear stuff. I just happened to be dusting the lamp in the living room and heard them talking in the dining room. It's not my fault they didn't know I was there listening. So, anyway, that's how I knew you were gay for sure," she admitted. "Though I always suspected since you used to steal my Barbie's."

"I didn't steal them, I borrowed them," I defended myself.

"Sure," she said.

"Did you overhear anything else?"

"No. Except maybe a name, Gary or maybe Larry..."

"Barry," I confirmed.

"That's it," she snapped her fingers. "Barry. But then they noticed me leaning my ear towards them, so they stopped talking."

"The nerve of them," I joked.

If there's one thing you need to know about Erika, it's that she is a snoop.

Relief must have shown on my face because she got that *'I'll dig it out of you'* look on her face.

"So, who is he? This Barry guy," she wanted to know.

"Non of your business. Just a guy, that's all."

"Not a boyfriend then?"

"Nope."

"Well, you'll tell me eventually," she said. "I have vays of making you talk," she said in her best German accent. "So, how about this Rick guy?"

I got up and started unpacking again.

"What about him?" I asked.

"He's hot. I had a crush on him for so long but then he got together with that Luke guy and knew I didn't have a chance. Luke is pretty hot too. Man, why are all the gay guys so hot?"

"I'm gay and I'm not hot," I said while placing some shirts in a drawer.

"Your hot, albeit in a different way from them. You have this cute innocence about you. Are you still a virgin? And since you're gay, vaginas don't count."

"Huh? I never had sex with a girl."

"Or boys?"

"You know," I had to laugh at her tenacity, "you sure are a nosy little brat, aren't you?"

"Nosy, yes. Brat? I take offense to."

"Well, then I apologize."

"I bet you had sex. It's a long drive from the bus station but not that long. It took y'all longer than it should have."

When I ignored her and continued to unpack, she took that as a yes."

"I knew it. Did you fuck each other? Who did what?"

"You seem far too interested in in my love life."

She shrugged her shoulders.

"I think two guys together is hot."

"Alright, I give up. If I tell you will you promise not to spread it around?"

"Sure, I might be nosy but I'm not a blabber mouth."

"Okay," I took a deep breath. "We sucked each other and that is all. He was the first guy I have ever been with. Now it seems he is back with Luke because they can't keep they're hands off each other and even though I just met him, I think I'm in love. But he will never love me the same way." It all gushed out of me in an angry storm.

"Gee, sorry. I didn't mean to pry."

I stared at her like she just dropped down from Venus.

I threw my suitcase in the closet and slammed the door shut. I knelt on the floor facing away from her, ashamed as if I told her my most dreadful secrets. She knelt beside me and encased me in a gentle embrace.

"I'm sorry," I said. "I just got carried away with all that. I didn't mean to say anything.

"It's alright, sweetie. Sometimes I don't know when to shut the fuck up. You really in love with Rick?"

"Maybe. Maybe it's just because he was my first. I fall in love too easily and the guy is never in love with me. Rick will never be in love with me. And Barry..."

"What about him?"

I shook my head violently.

"No. I'm not ready to talk about it. It was just a total mess and I want to forget about it."

"Sure. I understand," she patted my shoulder. "I won't pry any further, I promise. But if you ever need a friend to talk to, just remember I'm here for you."

"I'll remember," I put on a small fragile smile on my face. "Thank you."

"So," she stood up, wiping off her jeans, "I will let you rest after your long trip." She helped me up and gave me a sincere hug. "Don't worry, it will be alright. You're among friends and family."

With that, she left me to my nap.

Chapter Four

I had drifted off to sleep a few moments after Erika left when I heard a noise. My eyes darted open and thought it must have been a vivid dream. I closed them once more and was about to drift back to slumber when a door opened and closed. This time I looked up and saw this man standing at the door, his back to me. It appeared as though he was peeking out the door. He closed it again then turned towards me and jerked back, startled.

"What the hey, Dude!" He said, sounding alarmed.

"Um...hi. Uh...this is my room," I informed the intruder.

"Oh, you must be Hank's nephew," he said in understanding. "I'm Brad." He stuck out his hand for me to shake, I took it tentatively and he grasped hold of mine firmly in his. "Nice to meet you."

"Nice to meet you too. Um...can I ask you something?"

"Shoot."

"Um...what are you doing in my room?"

He started howling with laughter, then realized he might be making too much noise for whoever he was hiding from and stifled his glee. Looking around nervously.

"Oh, man. I didn't realize. I mean, I knew you were coming, but I just didn't think. This room is the guest room and it's usually empty. I'm playing hide and seek with Diego."

"Playing what with who?" I asked, puzzlement in my voice." Um...how old are you?"

He laughed again. Nice to see someone was amused by this.

"Twenty-one. But this is an adult version of the game. Who ever looses has to suck the winners dick. I lost twice in a row. Not that I mind. Diego has a great dick. But just thought it would be nice to win for once."

"Oh. I see," Brad was a nice looking fellow. Though more of a surfer type than a cowboy, yet somehow an interesting combination of the two, in his tight wrangler jeans, cowboy boots, and Hawaiian shirt. His long blond hair sleeked back as if fresh out of the shower. He smelled good too, like roses and peaches.

"In case he comes back this way, mind if I hide under the covers with you," Brad asked, desperately.

"Well...uh...I don't know."

"You're not naked under there are you?" He smirked.

"No!" I said loud enough for the whole house to hear.

"I think I hear him coming. Scoot over."

He gave me no choice as he lifted the covers and proceeded to climb in the bed, so I quickly shuffled to the other side. He promptly covered himself up when the bedroom door crashed open.

"Aha," he said. "Ah...oh...thought you were someone else." A handsome Latino man said who I assumed was Diego.

"Hey, no problem," Brad moved his fingers down to my crotch and held on, I jumped and squirmed at the intrusion.

"Is there anyone in there with you?" Diego asked, suspiciously, one eyebrow rising.

"Why do you ask?" I squeaked.

"Because," he came closer to the bed, "there is a big lump on this side." He pulled the covers back revealing Brad, curled up and fondling my crotch. "Aha!" Diego said again. "You know, you might have gotten away if you weren't trying to get into his pants."

Brad had his hand on my hardening cock, kneading it through the fabric of my jeans.

"I know. Just thought it might be fun to have a threesome before supper," Brad said, sheepishly.

"What?" I said, sitting up in my bed.

"You know you're up for it," Brad said to me. "Your dick is getting hard."

"You know the rules Brad. Gotta suck my cock. And since you were a co-conspirator," Diego's dark eyes looked at me, "you gotta help him."

I gulped.

"Listen. I'm just an innocent bystander. I don't know either of you"

"Doesn't matter. You gotta help him suck my dick," he said lustfully. "And we can get to know each other better."

No less than a couple hours ago I was a virgin. Now here I was with two hot studs who wanted me in a threesome. Diego began to strip by first unzipping his black pants while Brad leaned into me, kissing me. His tongue invaded my mouth. I laid there in shock, letting it happen, wanting it to happen. I got into the kiss and kissed him back. I watched Diego strip as Brad and I wrestled with each other's tongue. He took off his pants and boxer briefs at the same time, revealing first, his thick black bush, and then his long thick cock. Inch by inch. I estimated it must have been at least eight inches. He was uncut and it had a slight curve. It was beautiful.

Diego was every bit the Latin lover. He had dark bedroom eyes, golden brown skin, luscious full lips. His black hair was slicked back with gel. His body smooth except for the bushy hair above his dick. His ass was round like two melons. He had abs to die for and a killer chest. He spoke with a slight accent. In a word, he was sexy as hell.

"Okay Brad, break it up and come over here and suck some dick," he punctuated the order by slapping his hard curved dick against the palm of his hand.

Brad reluctantly left my swollen lips and slithered off the bed and onto his knees in front of Diego, who stood over him with a satisfied smile of triumph of winning another game of hide and seek.

Brad looked up into Diego's dark eyes and licked his lips. He moved forward, his tongue stretched out, and touched the tip to Diego's dickhead. Brad grabbed the base of the dick with one hand while clasping onto the fat balls with his other, then in one plunge he swallowed all of Diego's cock, down to the root. Diego moaned loudly as his dick was engulfed in the warmth of Brad's mouth over and over again.

"Oh yes, Brad!" Diego hissed. "You suck good man. You see why I love winning," Diego rubbed his fingers through Brad's hair. "Just for the pleasure of your lips around my dick. Oh yeah, suck it, man!"

Brad went to town on Diego's dick. Slobbering all over it from head to root. Diego had his hands behind his head, flexing his muscles, his legs were spread wide enjoying the sensations Brad was giving him. I watched from the bed, still stunned by the turn of events. I had to pinch myself to make sure I wasn't dreaming.

They had invited me to join but wasn't sure when I could jump in as Brad hogged Diego's dick for himself.

Brad finally pulled off Diego's dick, licked the head once more, and then looked back at me.

"Well? Come on. Help me suck this thing. There's plenty for two."

That was my cue, I guess. So, I hopped off the bed and knelt before the Latin heartthrob. He smiled down at me and placed his hand on top of my head, pushing me towards his leaking cock.

My mouth opened and he entered slowly, his dick touched my tongue sending flavors of salty pre-cum into my senses. His flesh was hard as steel. I wrapped my lips around it and he pushed even more into my watering mouth. I gagged a bit, but he pulled back before I had a choking fit. He pulled back out until his dickhead was right at my lips, then plunged back in. He was face fucking me slowly. In and out in and out.

"Dios mio." he breathed. "It feels so good. Your mouth is a really nice place for a big cock to be buried in" he said. I knew I was blushing, my face felt hot with a burning sensation. This was all new to me. "Okay, now really suck me," he stopped his fucking motions and I began sucking him in earnest, bobbing my head back and forth on his cock. Brad grabbed hold the back of my head and made sure to push it forward each time I moved back. "Mierda! Eres tan Bueno!" He shouted. I wasn't sure what he said, but I think it was a compliment.

"Why don't we move this to the bed," Brad suggested and lifted me to my feet, disconnecting my mouth from Diego's dripping cock.

"Sure," Diego agreed. "Everyone has to get naked. I feel like the odd man out." Diego pushed me back against the bed and I plopped down on the firm mattress. "Starting with you," he smiled, sexily.

Diego hurriedly undid my pants and yanked them off me along

with my underwear. My hard cock sprang out nearly hitting him in the eye. He laughed at the eagerness of my hard organ.

Meanwhile, Brad had unbuttoned my shirt and I lifted up so he could remove it. Now I was completely naked in front of these two hot studs.

Brad hurriedly pulled off his clothes while Diego plunged down on my dick.

"Oh my God!" I'm not sure I would ever get used to the sensation of my dick being sucked. It felt too damned good.

The bed shook as another body shuffled over to me. Brad was now undressed, his cock stuck straight out, hard and cut, at least seven inches. He straddled my face and sat down. His balls entered my watering mouth and my hand moved to his cock. I jerked it a few times before he leaned over my prone body. Diego pointed my cock towards Brad's hungry mouth and he engulfed it and sucked wildly on it while Diego moved down to my balls. Diego's mouth on my balls and Brad's sucking were driving me to unfathomable bliss, as the pleasure consumed my aching body.

As I chewed on Brad's balls, I decided to do some exploring. Spreading his ass cheeks, I started poking at his hole. He sucked on my dick even harder as he felt my fingers invade his insides. Diego kissed my thighs and moved down to my knees and then my feet. He licked my toes and sucked on them, one by one. I had no idea having my toes sucked would feel so good, and so sensual.

Diego moved back up my legs to my crotch. He held my dick at the base just as Brad had slid up to the head. Diego aimed my dick at his luscious mouth and dove back on it. Brad backed up a little so his dick could enter my mouth. While Brad was face fucking my face, Diego did a great job at sucking my cock.

"Let's each take a turn riding his cock," Diego lifted off my cock to say, still jerking it slowly. My cock was slick with pre-cum and saliva and pulsed with anticipation for sweet release.

"Cool idea, dude," Brad agreed.

Brad got up off my face.

"Wh-what are you going to do?" I asked nervously.

"Don't worry, you're going to enjoy this. But always remember, safety first," Diego went to get his jeans and pulled out his wallet. He found a condom. "Got some lube?" He asked Brad.

"Sure," Brad grabbed his jeans and pulled out a small bottle of lube and tossed it to Diego. These boys came prepared.

"This was supposed to be about me getting my dick sucked," Diego chuckled as he unwrapped his condom. "After all, I did win at hide and seek. But I'm flexible. This turned out to be something even more awesome. Have you ever fucked anyone?" I shook my head no. "Then you're in for a treat."

Diego rolled the condom over my dick while Brad squirted lube on his hands then rubbed it onto my dick, jacking me. Diego squatted over me and sat down on my dick, Brad held it as Diego spread his ass cheeks and the head of my dick went into his hole. He pushed down more, harder, until it was all in. It felt tight, warm, and incredible. He rose up and down fucking me with his back to me. I could see my dick buried between his glistening brown ass cheeks.

"Oh God!" I moaned.

"You like that, huh?" Diego asked as he lowered and raised himself on my rod.

"Yeah, he loves it. His eyes are glazing over," Brad snickered.

Now I understood what Diego meant by riding me. I felt ashamed for being so naïve, but I knew nothing of sex until recently. I thought about it and fantasied about it a lot. I was never sure it would ever happen. So, this was like a dream. A hot wet dream come to glorious life.

Diego continued riding me and I was ready to explode. Diego must have sensed this because he got up off me and unrolled the condom. Brad quickly replaced the old condom with a new one and it was Diego's turn to squirt the lube in his hand and rub it onto my dick. Brad opted to ride me facing front. Brad's face was a mixture of pain and pleasure. Diego bent down and took Brad's dick into his mouth and sucked hard as Brad bounced on my throbbing cock. I couldn't help but to lift my ass up from the bed and fuck into him, which plunged Brad's cock deeper into Diego's sucking mouth. It was almost like we were all of one body. Merged together for the ultimate orgasmic thrill.

"Oh God! Diego! I'm gonna cum! I'm gonna fucking cum!" Brad warned. Diego paid no heed and sped up his sucking. "Oh my God!" Brad froze, suspended in time, as he unleashed a torrent of cum into Diego's mouth. 'Ooh! Ah! Yes!" Diego swallowed most of it but some dribbled from his mouth. "Oh God!" Brad fell back, trying to regain his breathing. My cock slipped out of his hole still searching for its own rclcasc.

"Suck my cock," Diego said to me, "then we'll help you cum."

Diego sat on the edge of the bed as I knelt before him, looking into his brooding eyes, I saw lust there. In that moment, he wanted me, and I was more then willing to give him what I had. To give him the pleasure I had only just discovered. Slowly, achingly, I went down on his magnificent cock.

"Yeah! Suck my dick!" He ran his fingers through my hair as my head bobbed up and down. "Yeah! Oh God!" He held my head tighter as his orgasm overtook him. "Here it comes!" He grunted. "Gonna cum!" He gave me no choice but to swallow as he held my head down on his cock while cum shot out from his dickhead down my throat. I wasn't sure if I liked him cumming in my mouth, but the taste wasn't too bad. He let my head up and cum continued to ooze out of his prick and out of my mouth.

"Wow! You suck good, don't you?" I shrugged my shoulders. "Well, "come up here, it's your turn." He pulled me up onto the bed and laid me back.

Brad and Diego were on either side of me, taking turns jacking my cock and fondling my balls. A hand slid up and down my shaft, while another hand rolled my balls and pulled on them. Both guys leaned into me. It was a three-way kiss where all our lips touched.

Brad jerked my cock faster and I felt my sperm boiling from my balls into my cock.

"God! You're gonna make me cum!" I shouted.

"Well, that's the idea," Brad said.

Diego moved down and wrapped his lips around my dickhead as Brad masturbated me faster.

"Oh God! I'm gonna cum!" I shouted. "Oh God! Oh! Ah! Uh," I lifted my butt off the bed as cum blasted from my cock into Diego's mouth. He captured most but some leaked out onto Brad's hand. "Oh wow!" I slowly came down from my climax. "That was intense," I said.

"Sure was," Brad agreed and kissed me.

"Maybe you'll join us for a game of hide and seek sometime," Diego laughed.

"I'm sure I'll enjoy that."

"We all will," Brad said.

"About time for supper. Better get dressed and cleaned up." Diego suggested.

We all had put our jeans back on and were putting on our shoes when there was a gentle knock at the door. The person didn't wait for an answer before coming in.

It was Rick.

His eyes narrowed upon seeing Brad and Diego in my room.

"Supper is ready guys. Better hurry up," he turned to leave, then glanced back at me. "Hope you had fun, Phillip," his tone was clipped, and I wondered if I did something to upset him.

"Wonder what's eating his ass?" Brad asked as he and Diego ushered me out the door.

Chapter Five

Erika kept giving me meaningful looks during supper. Rick sat opposite me while Diego and Brad, the two men who had just squeezed the cum out of me not twenty minutes before, sat on either side of me. Rick seemed to be keeping a suspicious eye on the three of us as if he suspected what we did before he came in.

I stuffed myself with meatloaf, mashed potatoes, green beans, corn on the cob, and corn bread, trying to ignore Rick's leering eyes. My stomach felt like it was about to explode, so I stopped eating and wiped my mouth with a napkin. Luke sat next to Rick and he told some lame joke that had Rick howling with laughter. Suddenly, Rick had forgotten about me and what had happened in my room earlier. I felt a pang of jealousy as he and Luke whispered something back and forth. A secret shared between two lovers.

There were two more cowboys Uncle Hank introduced me to when I came down for supper. Jake and Todd.

Uncle Hank wasn't kidding; Jake was sexy as hell. His black skin was smooth and flawless, his lips full and voluptuous. His shirt opened enough to reveal some chest hair. His head was shaved, though shadowed with the regrowth of hair. He was movie star handsome and my dick tingled when I looked at him.

Todd was a handsome redhead who appeared to be in his late thirties. He had green eyes which seem to sparkle whenever he spoke. He had a barrel chest and thick arms from hours working on the ranch. When he smiled, he showed all his teeth, the two front teeth were slightly gaped.

"So, Phillip," Brad started, "where are you from?" He scooped a spoonful of mashed potatoes in his mouth and chewed suggestively.

"Dallas," I answered him.

"So, a Texas boy born and bred, eh?"

"Brad is from California," Diego put in. "He always wished he was a true Texan." I could tell Diego was teasing Brad. They had that kind of relationship it seemed; a mix of friends, lovers, and brothers all rolled into one.

"Yeah, but I had it good back in Cali. The surf, the sand, the sun, the hot guys," he sat back, crossed his arms, and thought for a second, "actually there's plenty of hot guys here too so I'm good." He began shoveling more food into his mouth.

Out of the corner of my eye, I noticed Rick's hand slip under the table into Luke's lap. Luke laughed and pulled Rick's hand away from him, with Rick having a sheepish look.

"Not at the table, Rick. Where's your manners," everyone hooted at that. Except for me. I sat with my arms crossed and pouted. It was getting harder to hide my feelings. I had to try though, so I uncrossed my arms and forced a smile upon my face.

Occasionally, Rick would cast a glance at me with a scowl on his forehead, as if he were upset with me. Then he would ignore me again and go back to chatting with Luke.

Erika had sympathy written all over her face as she witnessed my anguish. I tried to telepathically tell her to stop worrying and that I would be okay. It probably looked as if I was having a fit of some kind as I kept rolling and crossing my eyes trying to get the message across to the other end of the long table where she sat. Rick noticed and watched me with mouth agape for a few moments. Amusement twinkled in his eyes as he observed my awkward attempt to be psychically connected with Erika. His scowl no longer on his brow.

I halted my machinations when I saw him smiling at me. I folded my hands in my lap and looked down at my plate, a blush growing on my cheeks. Erika had found it all quite funny and couldn't help to indulge herself in a giggle.

Rosa, my uncle's housekeeper and Erika's mom, brought out plates with Apple pie and ice cream. She served me first since I was a special guest.

She worked for my uncle for as long as I could remember. Rosa and Erika lived in a small cottage on the ranch, Erika's dad had never been in the picture and I'm not sure whatever happened to him. Rosa would always make my favorite meal and dessert when I came for a visit. She out did herself with the meal she prepared tonight.

"Eat up Mister Phillip," Rosa told me, "You need to put meat on those bones."

"I think he has plenty of meat, don't you agree Diego?" Brad said, jokingly.

"Yup," Diego squeezed my thigh, "plenty of meat," he winked at me.

Erika sat there staring at us and suddenly comprehending the type of welcome I got from the two studs sitting next to me.

Rick's scowl seemed to have returned for a flash of a second, then disappeared.

"No. He's too skinny," Rosa insisted, missing the innuendo. "He needs to eat lots of my cooking."

"Yeah, he eats like a bird," Rick piped in, a little sourly.

"But I cleaned my plate," I said, defending myself.

"But you had small portions of everything," Rick countered. "And you hardly ate your cheeseburger at lunch."

"You had a cheeseburger for lunch?" Erika piped in. "Naughty boy," she winked at me, giggling.

"Well, I intend to help build your appetite up while you're here," Rick said. Erika spat her iced tea out and coughed. Rick realized how it sounded. "I mean...there's lots to do on the ranch...uh...work stuff."

"Alright, leave the boy alone," Uncle Hank spoke up. "With the work I'll give him, he'll soon be eating like a cowboy," he insisted, ignoring the sexual tension in the room.

"How 'bout we go and decorate the tree now," Clem said. He hadn't said anything all evening. He was a quiet and reserved man. I think he might have been shy, but he spoke up when he needed to. He had gray hair and sparkling blue eyes and was in excellent shape for a guy past sixty.

Everyone readily agreed with Clem and got up to head for the living room. I was about to get up when Rosa pushed me back down onto my chair.

"You finish your pie first," she demanded, looking cross.

"I'll finish it later," I said.

"No! Now!" She insisted. "I'll bring hot chocolate out in a few minutes. Now eat."

She went back into the kitchen as I grabbed my fork and began eating as fast as I could. I swore they were trying to fatten me up for Christmas dinner.

The lights were already strung up by the time I finished my pie. They were placing ornaments carefully along the tree, laughing and singing along with Christmas carols playing on the radio. Rick sat on the couch watching the festivities. His legs were spread wide apart and his arms were draped across the top of the couch.

I sat next to him and he looked in my direction, acknowledging my presence with a curt nod.

"Are you mad at me?" I asked, timidly.

"No. Why?"

"Well, it's just that...um...you've been acting funny, is all."

"Funny how?"

"Like you're mad at me or something."

"Well, I'm not. It just caught me off guard, that's all."

"What did?" I said, confused.

"You, Brad, and Diego. In your room, doing who knows what," he sounded bitter.

"You jealous?" I asked hopefully, maybe too hopefully. His head pivoted towards me with a strange look.

"Why would I be jealous?"

"Well, if that's not it...uh...oh, never mind." I sat back, folded my arms, and huffed. "I'm allowed to have sex with anyone I want since I'm unattached," I said, snidely.

He looked at me for a long moment making me uncomfortable with his steely gaze.

"I'm gonna help with the tree," he finally said. "You coming?"

"Sure," I said, begrudgingly. We went to grab some ornaments from a box and went about to find a place on the tree for them.

All the decorations and tinsel filled the tree with beauty and wonder. Everything was done except for the star my uncle held in his hand. He strained his neck looking up at the tall tree.

"I reckon one of you young fellas should put this here star on top. I'm getting too old to do it myself," he said

"It's a mighty tall tree," Luke said. "Maybe if I pick Rick up." He locked his arms around Rick, cupping his hands at Rick's firm jean covered ass, trying to lift him up.

"Hey, enough of that!" Rick admonished. "If anyone's gonna do the lifting it's gonna be me." It was Rick's turn to try and lift Luke. Luke and Rick were both laughing their asses off as one tried to grab the other. It made me want to puke my dinner up.

"You okay?" Erika whispered in my ear.

"Yeah. Didn't you get my message?" I asked.

"No. What message?"

"My psychic one."

"Oh. Is that what you were trying to do? I thought you were having a bad reaction to the meatloaf."

"Okay boys, break it up," my uncle stepped in. "Why don't we give the honors to Phillip."

All eyes were on me and I felt heat rising to my face.

"I'm too short," I said quietly.

"You can get on Rick's shoulders," Clem suggested.

"Good idea," Erika spoke up.

"Or he could get on mine," Diego suggested.

"Rick's taller. We could use all the height we can get," Uncle Hank reasoned.

"What about a ladder?" Rick asked.

"It's out in the shed. This will be quicker, then we can have the cocoa and look at the lights."

Rick got on all fours on the floor, his perky jean clad ass facing me, he looked over his shoulder, with a mischievous smile.

"Okay, get on," he said.

"Hmm. There's something sexy about a submissive cowboy," Erika interjected.

"Erika!' Rosa exclaimed, having overheard her daughter as she brought in the mugs of hot cocoa.

"Well, there is," she said defiantly.

"What am I going to do with you," Rosa said, shaking her head.

"I'm not sure that will work," I told Rick. "Maybe you should kneel on the floor in front of the couch and I can get on that way."

Rick moved over to the couch and I got on the cushions and straddled his shoulders.

"Ready? Hold on," Rick said.

Rick got up off the floor slowly, I held onto his neck for dear life, finding myself swaying as he lifted to a standing position. I didn't weigh much so it wasn't much of a struggle for him and he was big and strong. Uncle handed me the star and we headed toward the tree. I had to bend the branch down a bit to fit the star on it. Everyone admired the star as Clem flipped a switch. The house lights went out while the tree lights went up in colorful, sparkling majesty.

I felt a hand on my ass and when I looked down to see who it was, surprise was an understatement as I discovered it was Todd, the redheaded cowboy. He winked at me and turned his attention back at the tree.

"I think you can let me down now," I told Rick.

"Oh sorry. You were so light I didn't realize you were still there."

He lowered himself on the floor and I got off.

Suddenly, Luke jumped on Rick while he was still down on the floor and tackled him. They rolled around and wrestled, trying to pin the other down with brute force, and both were giddily laughing. Rick managed to roll Luke over and be on top of him, crotch to crotch, and held him down. It was an erotic scene watching two big handsome cowboys in such an intimate position. They looked into each other's eyes and the pang of jealousy returned. I fought it off. I only met Rick and had no right to hope there could be something between us. And there were some other cowboys here who were more than willing to fulfill my needs.

"Give?" Rick asked Luke.

There was a long pause. Christmas music filled the quiet air, and Christmas lights added a soft glow to the room. I sat on the couch watching the two cowboys. Their crotches rubbed lightly together as Rick held down his lover.

"Well?" Rick asked, tightening his hold.

"I'm thinking, I'm thinking," Luke said. Everyone started laughing. "I kinda like this closeness," he said, seductively.

Rick lifted himself up and looked down at Luke with a big grin.

"Well, I won then, didn't I?"

"Yes, Rick. You always win," Luke agreed.

Rick offered him his hand and helped Luke up.

"Is it always like this around here?" Jake asked. He hadn't been talking much at dinner, but seemed quite amused by all the activities, as if observing the mating habits of the homosexual.

"The boys can get pretty rowdy sometimes," Uncle Hank said. "There are times when I have to put a hose on them to make them quit humping each other," he said with a chuckle.

"Now Hank," Clem said. "You know we were the same when we were young."

"We still are, Clem," my uncle gave his partner a peck on his lips. "Though not quite as rowdy. But we still make some noises like two wolves howling in the night."

"Hank!" He gave my uncle a playful slap on the knee. "Not in front of the children."

Todd sat next to me and stretched out an arm over the couch.

"I can get pretty rowdy myself," he leered at me.

"The tree sure is beautiful," Luke said as he and Rick stood, admiring the beauty of the twinkling lights aglow, sparkling off the ornaments.

"Yup," Rick agreed. "Makes me want to sing," he smiled, mischievously. "Jingle bells, jingles bell, jingle all the way."

Luke sung the next part.

"Oh, what fun it is to ride Santa on his sleigh, hey! And guess who's gonna be Santa," Luke said to Rick, getting behind him, and started humping.

"Hey, do I have to pull the hose out on you two?" My uncle warned.

"Hey," Rick said, "you know I'm the one always on top," they switched places and Rick was humping Luke.

"Clem, get the hose," Uncle Hank teased.

"Oh yeah, give it to me Santa," Luke said, his eyes rolling back, his tongue sticking out.

Even though they both were fully dressed, it looked very sexy to see them dry humping each other. But that jealousy still nagged at me and didn't seem to want to let go. I wanted to go to bed. I never did get to take that nap.

"Is it just me or is it getting hot in here?" Jake asked. I could have sworn there was a growing bulge inside his jeans.

"I think I'm going to go to bed," I announced to no one in particular.

"But it's still early," Brad said.

"Yeah, but I had a long day."

"Good night, amigo," Diego said, hugging me as I got up from the couch, I felt Todd staring at my ass.

"Good night Pip," Erika gave a quick one-armed hug, as she held a mug with the other hand. "We'll go riding tomorrow."

"Gosh, I haven't gone riding since I was eight."

"I know. It's as easy as riding a bike. Only, it has legs instead of wheels."

I said my good nights and headed for my room. I also needed a quick shower, the scent of sex lingered on me. Suddenly, I became worried everyone had noticed, but I put that thought aside as I stripped.

Chapter Six

As I soaped my naked body in the shower, I contemplated all that took place that day. I had sex with three gorgeous cowboys. Never thought anything like that would ever happen to me. I must admit I always had a thing for cowboys. Their sexy ruggedness really turned me on, and Rick was the king of the cowboys in my mind. If there was something I wanted for Christmas, it would be Rick underneath the Christmas tree completely naked, with a big red bow tied around his neck.

The water washed away the soap from my smooth body but couldn't wash away thoughts of Rick from my mind. *Why was I so hung up on him,* I wondered.

When I turned off the shower, I heard the distinct sound of rushing water. Someone was in the bathroom. I peeked around the shower curtain and saw Rick there at the commode with his dick in his hand, peeing.

"Um...this bathroom is occupied, you know," I informed him.

"Sorry, but I had to pee really bad."

"Don't you have one in the bunk house?" I asked.

"Yup, but someone was using it. And I had to go bad. I doubt your uncle would have wanted me to use his and Clem's. Besides, I thought you went to bed." He shook his dick and stuffed it back inside his jeans and zipped up.

"Had to shower first. Didn't get a chance earlier." I thought for a moment and realized something. "Hey, there's a half bath downstairs. You could have used that one."

"Oops, I forgot," he shrugged as he washed his hands at the sink and dried them with a hand towel. He looked back at me with a knowing smile. "You got distracted there by Diego and Brad."

"Huh?"

"They were in your room," he rolled his eyes. "That's the reason you didn't get a chance to take a shower before supper, isn't it?" He said it calmly, yet it felt like an accusation.

"Would you mind handing me that towel," I did my best to ignore his last comment.

"Sure." He tossed me the towel he was using.

"Not the hand towel!" I said, tossing it back to him. "That one over there," I pointed to the large bath towel hanging on the back of the door.

"Oh, sorry." He handed me the bigger towel. "You know; I've seen you naked. Hell, I even had that thing in my mouth. So why so modest now?"

I blushed red all over.

"Golly. I ain't never seen anyone turn red so quickly all over their body before."

"Would you mind leaving, please? I just want to get into my pj's and go to bed. Been a long day."

"Don't I know it," he granted me with another one of his drop-dead gorgeous smiles. "Sure thing. And oh, sorry if I've been a little crabby since I found you in your room with those two. As I said, I was just taken aback is all. If I gave you a hard time, sorry."

"That's alright," I smiled, letting him know I meant it, and I think I did.

"Well, good night, Phillip."

***

A sound tapping against my window woke me from a dreamless sleep. It was after two in the morning as I looked at my digital clock with half opened eyes, I'd been asleep for nearly five hours. I thought at first it might be hail knocking persistently against the glass, but it had been clear all day with no signs of oncoming storms.

I groggily sat up in my bed and threw my legs over one side as I listened to the soft tap and then another. I could have sworn I heard a distant chant of my name from somewhere below. I rubbed my eyes, stretched my arms, and yawned. Then, as softly as I could, tiptoed over to the window and looked out. A figure of a man stood there in the shadows with something in his hand he was readying to throw, until he saw me squinting out the window.

"Can you come out to play?" He asked, quietly. It was Todd.

"What are you doing?" I asked, feeling awkward, and a little like Juliet being courted by Romeo.

"Trying to get you up?" He whispered loud enough for me to hear.

"It's the middle of the night."

"Can you come down? We can just talk if you want. Look at the stars. It's a lovely night."

Instead of standing there arguing with him, I made the decision of going down to talk. He seemed lonely and needed someone to talk to.

"Alright. Be right down," I called to him.

As I stepped out into the night, he was right there on the porch, casually swinging on the porch swing.

"Beautiful night, ain't it?" He smiled at me as I sat beside him.

"Yup," I agreed. There must have been an endless number of stars in the sky. The moon was crescent and there were no clouds to hinder the view. "So, what did you want to talk about?"

"Okay, I'm just gonna lay it all out there for you. I'm horny as hell and my hand just won't cut it anymore. I thought maybe you could help a guy out."

"What makes you think I would? Help you out, that is."

"Well, I seen the way Brad and Diego been flanking around you, getting cozy. And I seen the way you look at Rick."

"Very observant, aren't you."

"Yup. Suppose I am. Don't mean to put you in an awkward position, but just thought I'd ask is all. It doesn't have to be a thing. I know you have your eye on Rick."

"I don't know what..."

"I told you," he cut me off with a wave of his hand. "I seen the way you look at him. I know it's not just lust, I'm pretty sure you love him."

"I haven't known him for long. How could it be love?" I wasn't really asking him; I was asking the universe.

"Boy, I've seen true love grab hold of someone quicker than a rattle snake."

"That's a delightful thought."

He chuckled and shook his head.

"Well, it's the truth. Maybe you two are soul mates and he just don't know it yet. Sometimes that happens," he shrugged. "You just have to wait and see if he realizes it before you two are old graying men with walkers."

"What if Luke and Rick are the soul mates and I'm just an interloper. What if I don't matter in the long run."

"Oh, you matter. You're here for a reason. Everyone has a purpose. You'll find yours someday. Usually it's right under your nose the whole time. Everyone you meet you touch in some special way; you leave a little of you behind in them and they walk around with a little piece of you."

"Wow, profound," I said.

"Maybe," he chuckled and shook his head again, grinning like a child at Christmas. "Or maybe I'm full of shit."

"I doubt that. I think you must be a wise old soul."

"Well," he got up from the swing and arched his back in a stretch. "It's getting late. If you don't want to do anything, might as well go to bed and get some shut eye."

I stood up and moved along side him.

"I didn't say I didn't want to do anything. In fact, I want to. I don't have a boyfriend so I'm free to do as I please."

"You sure?" He looked me in the eye as if trying to gauge my willingness.

"Yup. You're a mighty fine-looking man, Todd."

"Aw, well," he kicked at some pebbles on the porch, "thank you kindly."

"So, um...where would you like to do it?"

"Here," he stuck his hand out for me to take. "I'll show you a nice cozy spot around the back I think would be perfect."

He took me around the back of the house and up to an old wooden shack which was situated about a hundred feet from the house. It stood near a wooded area and sat far enough away from the bunkhouse and the main house to where we knew we would have some privacy.

I remember the shack from childhood. It had been built long before I was born. Erika and I used to play hide and seek, and I would often find a discreet place to hide inside the shack where it sometimes took her hours to finally figure out where I had been hiding. Once I knew she found my hiding spot, I had to find someplace new.

As we entered the old musty building, I told Todd about the games Erika and I would play.

He switched on a battery-operated lantern, casting a soft glow in the darkened shack.

"Yeah, I guess it would be a good hiding place if no one knew where to look," he said, taking off his hat and hanging it on the back of a wooden chair. "A lot of the cowboys come in here to get their rocks off."

"What?" I said in surprise, eyes widening picturing the hot sweaty cowboys fucking each other in the dark recesses of the shack.

"Yup. I heard them nick name it the 'love shack."

"Wow. Anyone I know?"

"Well, I don't know who started it. But I know of a lot of cowboys used it for that purpose. Including Luke and Rick."

Oh, I didn't need to hear that, I thought.

"Let's get naked and I'll show you how the 'love shack' got its name," he stripped off his shirt, revealing a mat of reddish blond hair covering his chest.

"You are rock solid," I admired his chest and abs, running my fingers across his six-pack. I slowly took off my shirt, ashamed of my body in comparison to his. "I'm afraid I still have some baby fat."

"Nonsense," he appraised my body. "You have the perfect body. Smooth, soft, yet firm, not fat, and yet not skinny. Aw, to be young again."

"You're not old," I argued.

"I'm about twenty years older than you."

"It doesn't matter," I said as I dropped my pants and underwear, revealing my hard cock. "Tonight, we're just two men who will have sex in an old shack."

"My word," he dropped to his knees. "" Your cock is just so...," he looked up at me, pleading with his eyes. "May I?"

"Of course."

He grabbed my cock at the base and stuck his tongue out and lapped at the juices forming on the head. I involuntarily moaned as his wet tongue made contact with the sensitive, slimy knob.

"What a tasty prick you have there, young man." He stood up and embraced my trembling, naked body. He kissed my lips and invaded my mouth with his tongue. I tasted myself on him. "Sit down in that chair over there and I will do you proper," he ordered.

I went over to a dark corner where a red homemade chair had been placed. I sat and removed my pants and underwear from my ankles, spreading my legs wide, an invitation for Todd to get to work.

He once again knelt and took my shaft in his strong rough hand, while running his other hand on my thigh. He moved his face closer as he opened his mouth, my cock throbbed in anticipation. My cock went into his warm mouth, his tongue lathed the head and slid down to the base as my cock disappeared inside him. My breath caught in my throat and I gurgled as his lips wrapped around my cock and he slid back up to the head and back down. It all seemed to happen in slow motion. But time had sped up again as he bobbed his head up and down. The sensations of his sucking making my legs twitch and my chest heave.

My explosion was imminent, but he stopped before my seed could gush into his mouth. He stood up and shucked his jeans off. He wasn't wearing underwear which surprised me for some reason.

I was fascinated by his red bush of hair above his dick. I had never seen a redhead naked before. He had a long, uncut dick, the head of his cock peeked out of the foreskin. My mouth watered at the sight of him and my dick jerked, sputtering pre-cum on my abdomen.

We quickly switched places. I munched on his big juicy balls and licked my way up his cock, to the purple head. I sucked on the head, slurping his pre-cum down my gullet. I sucked him down more than halfway until I began to gag, and then pulled back up to the head. I tried again, determined to go all the way down to his red pubes. His fingers ran through my hair, encouraging me.

"Oh yeah," he moaned as I sucked him. "You don't have to suck the whole thing, just do the best you can," he said when I tried once more to swallow his cock.

"But I need the practice," I got off his cock to tell him, going back to lick the head, making him quiver with need.

"I got a feeling you're going to get enough practice soon enough," he stood up from the chair and pulled me up from where I had been kneeling, embracing me in a tight hug while his lips devoured mine and our cocks touched one another, mine just below his.

He gently moved me over to where an old thin mattress lay on the dusty floor, and pushed me down on it, we both knelt, kissing, rubbing our hands over naked flesh.

"You want to fuck me?" He pulled away from kissing me to ask.

"I don't know," I said breathless. "Maybe you should fuck me."

"I think you want to save that for someone special."

I did.

"Okay, how do you want to do it?"

"Doggy style," he said. "And if you like, you can pretend I'm Rick."

I smiled at his thoughtfulness. He knew I really wanted Rick. My brain told me I may never have Rick, yet my heart told me not to give up, it was only a matter of time.

"No need to pretend," I told Todd. "Right here in this moment, it's only the two of us."

He handed me some lube he had taken from his jeans pocket, and a condom. He got on all fours and presented me his luscious ass. His cheeks spread a bit and I saw his hole. My cock throbbed with the beat of my heart.

I ripped the condom packet open and rolled it on my hard member, then lubed his hole and my cock, and inched forward to his entrance.

"Don't worry about being gentle. I can take it hard and rough," he said.

I took him at his word as I slammed into him with one thrust. He cried out and grunted but then after a second, he told me to fuck him hard. I moved my hips back slowly, then slammed into him again. I picked up speed with each thrust, going in and out. His ass was tight and gripped my cock like a vise.

"Oh God!" I screamed out. My hands held onto his hips as I fucked his firm cowboy ass. His pale skin shimmered from the lantern hanging on the wall. I could feel Todd's dick and balls swing below him as I thrust in and out of his hole. "I'm going to cum!" I shouted.

"Do it, boy. Cum in my tight hole," Todd encouraged me.

After a few more strokes in an out, my juices bubbled from my balls and up my dick.

"Oh God! Oh God!" My cum gushed out of my dick and filled the condom. I kept pumping as Todd's ass squeezed out the last drops of seed. I panted and leaned over his back to kiss his neck. I reached under him and realized he hadn't cum yet. His dick was hard as steel and wet and sticky with pre-cum. "It's your turn now."

I had him lie on his back, his legs spread out wide, his dick sticking straight up, his balls hanging low. I dove in and swallowed as much of his cock as I could, sucking, and bobbing my head, making haste to finish him off.

"Oh God, Phillip! I'm cumming!" His hands held onto my head and his cock pulsed out rope after rope of cum, Filling my mouth. "Ah! Ooh!"

He lay there, out of breath. His softening cock slipped out of my mouth. I had swallowed some of his cum, but a lot of it drizzled out from my mouth and onto his furry belly.

"That was something," he said after a moment of silence, with a glazed look in his eyes.

"It was," I crawled over him and lowed myself on top of him. Our soft cocks touched as our lips connected.

"If you weren't so hung up on Rick, I might make this a regular thing."

"If Rick and I never happen, which is more than likely, then maybe we could someday. Maybe I'll give it a year."

"True love is worth waiting for," Todd said with sad eyes, "you should never give up on it. Don't put a time stamp on it. You might get it sooner or later. Some folks get it sooner and some folks, like myself, may get it later."

"Maybe your time is coming then," I said.

"Or maybe it's too late."

"Like you said, it's never too late."

I kissed him once more then got up. We dressed and he turned the lantern off. We walked into the starry night knowing soon it will be dawn. We went our separate ways.

As I entered the house, it was quiet. When I saw the time, I almost panicked, it was almost five in the morning. No one seemed to be up but going back to sleep seemed a useless idea since I would have to get up within an hour.

At least I had good five hours of sleep, I thought as I curled up on my bed, thinking it wouldn't hurt if I just rested my eyes for a bit.

Chapter Seven

Something soft brushed against my cheek. At first, I thought it might have been a fly, then the thought occurred to me it might be a bug of some kind, or heaven forbid, a spider!

I shot up, flapping my hand on my cheek, making sure nothing was there. I heard soft laughter and movement on my bed. I flung my head in the direction of the culprit and found Rick sitting beside me with a feather in his hand.

"Time to get up, sleepy head," he snickered.

"Jerk," I said. The sun had come up and brightened the room. I realized I must have dozed off and slept longer than intended. "What time is it?" I asked.

"It's about eight."

"Oh gee," I started to get up, "is my uncle mad?"

"No. But Rosa is peeved you haven't gotten up to eat breakfast yet. It's getting cold."

"Oh gee. Really?" I felt bad about letting everyone down.

"Nah," he said, smirking. "We let you sleep in. Everyone figured you must have been tired from the long journey yesterday."

I breathed a sigh of relief and then started to get mad and pushed off my bed in a huff in search of fresh clothes in my closet.

"Why are you so mean?" I whined.

"Hey, I ain't mean. I'm just teasing you a little is all."

"Well, I really thought everyone would be mad at me. I know how early y'all get up on this ranch. And I'm sure uncle has some work for me to do." I pulled out a pair of black jeans from a hanger and decided on a red western styled shirt.

"Ain't nobody's mad at you. In fact, your uncle said you don't have to work today since it's your first full day here. He thought it best that you acclimate yourself first. So, you can go down and eat a leisurely breakfast, go riding with Erika, maybe go see a movie at the Old

Majestic. Whatever you please."

"Erika did want to go riding today. I would love to see some of our old haunts."

"Well, there you go."

Rick sat on my bed as I was about to unzip my pants. He eyed my crotch as he licked his lips. He was teasing me again. I shook my head and placed my hands on my hips.

"Do you mind? I need to get dressed."

"You're already dressed. Did you sleep in your clothes last night?"

"Ah, well...maybe," I stammered as I looked down at my attire from yesterday. "I need to get changed, then."

"Don't mind me," he lay on my bed, staring at the ceiling. "We're both boys here. It ain't nothing I ain't seen before."

For some reason, I felt shy having to get changed in front of him.

"Well, suit yourself. Just don't go looking at me change. This isn't a peep show, and you're not putting a dollar bill in my G-string," I reminded him.

I turned around, not able to face him as I unzipped my jeans. I pushed them down and bent over to take them off when I heard a whistle. I briskly spun around to see Rick's eyes still glued to the ceiling, acting innocent.

"Rick!"

"Yup?"

"You didn't peek, did you?"

"Would I do that? I just whistled at a pretty fly on the ceiling. The prettiest fly I ever did see."

***

"Now you sit and eat, Mister Phillip. Before you and Erika go out and play."

I had to smile at that.

"We're not kids anymore, Rosa. We're going riding." I informed her.

"You still kids to me. But no matter what, you need to eat before you go out."

"Yes, ma'am," I acquiesced to her demand.

"Hot stuff coming through," Erika said as she pushed the swinging door to the kitchen open, carrying two plates. "Thought I'd wait for you to get up so we can eat together and gossip before we go on our ride."

"You and your gossip," Rosa threw her hands up as if asking God what she should do with a headstrong child like Erika. "I'll get the orange juice. You two sit and eat," she pointedly looked at Erika, aiming a finger at her, "And no funny business."

"What do we have to gossip about?" I asked as Erika placed a plate in front of me.

"Oh, this and that," she sat across from me and scooped up some scrambled eggs in her fork, stuffing it in her mouth. "Let's start with you and Todd in the shack last night."

"What?" I gasped.

"Got up last night to pee and saw you heading out, so I snuck downstairs and peeked out the living room window. Saw Todd and you talking. I went back up and looked out my bedroom window where I saw you two sneaking off to the shack."

"Gosh, can't anyone have some privacy around here?" I wondered out loud as I stuffed my mouth with sausage.

"So, what were you and Todd doing? As if I didn't already know."

Heat flashed on my cheeks leaving a scarlet tinge.

"I refuse to answer that on the grounds it might make me sound like a slut."

Rosa came in and set two glasses and a pitcher of orange juice down. She left without saying a word. I wasn't sure if she had overheard me as her eyes avoided contact.

"What about Rick?"

"What about him?" I poured orange juice into a glass.

"Thought you loved him."

"I'm pretty sure he and Luke are getting back together. And I can't compete with someone like Luke. Have you seen him?"

"Aw, yes. If only I was a gay man," she looked dreamily up at the ceiling. "But that's neither here nor there. They have been apart for three years. That's a long time. They might have grown apart. Got on with their lives. Gotten over each other."

"They might have also missed each other madly and found they couldn't live without each other."

"Whose side are you on? Yours or Luke's?"

"Maybe I just believe in true love. How long were they together anyway before Luke split?"

"I think about two years. Not too long."

"But that's long enough for two people to fall in love," I stabbed some of my eggs with my fork and scooped them into my mouth.

"If Luke really loved Rick, he wouldn't have left," she reasoned. "And Rick would have gone with him if he loved Luke."

"Yeah, maybe. But I'm not gonna hold my breath."

Once we finished eating we went out to the stables to retrieve the horses for our ride. Erika went to a beautiful black horse.

"Phillip, meet Oscar."

"Oscar? You named your horse Oscar?" I said, bewildered.

"Sure. Oscar is a fine name."

"Yeah, but I thought it would be like Black Beauty or something."

"Already taken. I actually call him Ossie for short."

"Okay. Which horse am I riding?" I saw three more horses in the stable. I had my eye on a brown horse with a white stripe down its forehead. It looked strong and fast, maybe even a little wild. "I like that one," I told Erika, going up to it.

"That one? Get real," she giggled. "That horse would knock you off her so fast you would barely feel your ass on the saddle. Besides, that horse is Rick's. He might not appreciate you riding his horse. Cowboys and their horses are like sacred."

"If you say so," I shrugged.

"You're going to ride that one," she pointed to a smaller grayish horse which looked as if it had seen better days.

***

"Can't this thing go any faster," I complained as we rode our horses down a dirt trail.

"Nope," she said smiling, watching me struggle to stay in the saddle even at the slow pace we were going. "You're a little rusty, ain't ya?"

"I haven't been on a horse since I was eight.

"I think she likes you, so just relax and you will get reacquainted with riding."

"What's her name again?"

"Wilma, as in Flintstone."

"Wilma, huh?" I shook my head in amusement. "Who named her?"

"I did," she said defiantly. "when I was nine. The Flintstones was my favorite show."

"Oh, okay. No offense. But it seems that Blaze is the only horsy name around here. I don't think of horses when I think of Oscar or Wilma."

"If you had a dog would you name it Fido? Sometimes you gotta throw in an unexpected name otherwise we would have a stable full of Lightnings or Blazes."

"Point taken. And actually, I had a cat."

"What was its name?"

"Fluffy."

She didn't say another word, she just smirked knowingly.

We rode in silence for a while and I admired the scenery. West Texas has a more arid climate than Dallas, so it was unlikely we would have a white Christmas. It was rare to have a white Christmas in Dallas, for that matter. But we did get a lot of rainfall at times and colder temperatures.

The sun blazed high in the sky and it had to be somewhere in the eighties. I could feel the heat on me like a hot iron. I had the little black dainty hat I was wearing tilted over my eyes as we were riding towards the sun.

It looked more desert for miles around than what I was used to. I saw no houses nor buildings, just mountains and dirt, and blue sky.

And a white truck.

It seemed to have come out of nowhere, dust flying through the dry air as it came rushing towards us and made an abrupt halt. I could see there were two men in the truck. One of them rolled down his window and stuck his head out. He looked to be in his mid-twenties and had thick wavy black hair. He seemed like he could be the town's football hero as he was brawny and very handsome.

"Hey, pretty thang, how's it going?" He spoke with a thick Texas drawl. I thought he was talking to Erika as she was the only pretty thing...or, excuse me, thang...around here. So, I waited upon my little horse to see how this played out. "Hey, cutie, I'm talking to you. The one in the black hat."

I looked at Erika and saw she was wearing a turquoise hat.

"Yeah, you," he continued. "Erika, ain't he got a tongue on him?"

"Now Randy, he's just a little flustered, he ain't used to being called pretty."

"Well, is that right? He better get used to it cause he's prettier than a church bell chiming on a Sunday morn. Ain't that right Seth?" He asked the other guy in the truck.

"Yup. Sure thang."

Seth was just as hot as Randy, with shoulder length light brown hair.

"Now boys. You're embarrassing Phillip here."

They were. My face wasn't red from the sun.

"Tell you what, um...Phillip is it?" Randy said. "We'd like to invite you out with us tonight. We're going to Big Rob's, it's a honky-tonk here in town. A real jumping place. And we'll loosen you up real good."

"He'd love to," Erika said before I had a chance to say no.

"Great then. We'll pick you up around seven thirty. You staying at the South Bend Ranch?"

"He sure is," once again, Erika spoke for me "Hank's he's uncle."

"Aw, that's cool. Hank's a great guy. See you then, Phillip."

They drove off in a powder keg of dust.

"Why did you agree to that?" I asked as the horses began moseying at a slow pace once again.

"You need to get out. And you need to do something to get your mind off Rick."

"But a honky-tonk?"

"Don't they have them in Dallas?"

"Not sure. I've never been any place like that before."

"Could be fun. You won't know unless you try."

A jackrabbit suddenly jumped in the middle of the trail. We stopped to let it pass. I took of my hat and swiped a bead of sweat from my forehead.

"I'm mighty thirsty," I said. "Maybe we should stop and have some water."

We sat in the shade of a huge boulder and drank our bottled waters. It was refreshing and cooled me down quite a bit. Erika couldn't keep still once she drank her water. She went out and did cartwheels, somersaults, and handstands. I never was any good at that sort of thing, though I often tried. She got me to go out there with her and I did my best to do a cartwheel, but I'm sure it resembled more a pathetic lopsided spin.

We ran around chasing each other like we were kids again playing 'you're it.'

After playing in the sun for what seemed like an hour, we gave the horses some water and got back on and went on our merry way. Laughing and teasing each other, Erika especially teased me about my miserable attempt as a gymnast.

"I've never been any good at anything. Not really good." I admitted.

"Oh, I'm sure you must be good at something. You just have to find what it is and do it no matter what."

We came upon a fenced in area and two men were mending it where it had come loose from the posts. I recognized Rick right away, and Luke was with him. We were still quite a distance from them, so they didn't spot us right away.

They were talking in low whispered voices to one another and suddenly Luke pushed Rick against the post. It almost looked as if they were about to fight. But instead of fists pummeling each other, their lips smashed together, and they were in a passionate embrace. Their crotches ground together as their hands roamed their backsides.

Jealousy and arousal together is an odd thing.

"Sorry you had to see that, Phillip," Erika said. "But that is so hot."

Luke saw us coming first and broke away from the kiss.

"Howdy," he said, taking off his hat and waved at us with it.

Rick turned to see who it was coming up. When he saw it was us, he looked a little remorseful, like a lover had just caught him cheating. Only, he wasn't cheating, he was with his boyfriend, Luke.

"Hi Erika, Phillip," he nodded at us. "Having fun on your ride."

"Oh yes. But not as fun as you two, apparently," Erika said, smirking.

"We just took a brief break is all," Luke said.

"So, um...," Rick looked down at his boots as if trying to find something to say. "What are you two going to do for the rest of the day?"

"Oh," Erika started, "We're going to go and see a movie at the Old Majestic later this afternoon. They're showing It's a Wonderful Life."

"Oh, I love that movie. We should go Rick. It would be a lot of fun."

"Yeah, I guess it would," Rick admitted. "Hank said we just need to mend this here fence and then we might be able to take off for the day, so we better hurry up and finish then."

"The more the merrier," Erika gushed. "Then we might head over to DQ and then Phillip here has a hot date."

"A date?" Rick looked up at me with surprise. "With who?"

Did he sound jealous? I wondered. I hoped.

"It's not a date," I denied. "A couple of guys asked me to go to a honky-tonk with them is all. I think their names are Randy and Seth," I recalled.

"Randy and Seth?" Rick said with disgust. "They're a couple of rowdy guys. I don't think it would be good for you to get mixed up with those two."

"Aw, come on, Rick. The boy is eighteen. Stop big brothering him," Erika demanded.

Brothering?

"I'm sure he will be fine, Rick," Erika stuck up for me.

"Yeah," Luke said. "Let's get back to work so we can catch that movie," he suggested.

"Alright," Rick said, begrudgingly. Somehow, I knew he wanted to say more. I'm not sure what, but he looked like a guy who had something stuck in his craw.

Chapter Eight

The small theater's lobby was packed with people wanting to see the charm of the old Christmas favorite. Erika and I waited in line at the refreshment counter for the buttered popcorn and sodas we so craved. We had already gotten our tickets from the friendly middle-aged woman who wore horn rimmed cat glasses and a beehive and had dark red lipstick staining her lips. She looked as if she still lived in the sixties.

I began to wonder if Rick and Luke were going to make it when I didn't see them anywhere, until I saw them enter looking sweaty and worn out from a hard day's work.

"Glad to see you two made it," Erika greeted them.

"We almost didn't," Luke grumbled. "Rick's truck broke down and I was trying to fix it and was under the hood when this blockhead here," he gestured to Rick, "finally figured out he forgot to fill it with gas. So, we had to walk to the gas station and walk back."

"I said I was sorry," Rick said. "Guess I had other things on my mind."

"Well, it's just been a long day and I'm tired. So, let's just forget about it, okay? I'm sorry I yelled."

"Well, I'm sorry I forgot the gas," Rick said softly.

I hoped they weren't planning on making up right here in the Old Majestic's lobby.

"Well, everyone can have an off day," Luke got closer to Rick and was about to push in for a kiss.

"Well, let's get some popcorn and sodas and then everyone can be happy," Erika piped in.

Rick had pulled away from the almost kiss and pulled out some money from his pocket, slapping it on the counter.

"The treats on me," he winked at me. I almost melted like the butter on the popcorn but tried my best to hold it together. Rick always seem to make me tingle all over.

In the dark theater, James Stewart and Donna Reed flickered on the screen. A romantic scene with them walking home from some do came up and made me desire for some spark of my own. I caught a glimpse of Luke taking hold of Rick's hand. Rick casually slipped his hand from under Luke's and got his soda to take a sip. I munched my popcorn, keeping an eye on them for a few moments, wishing I had what they had, wishing I had what Luke had...Rick.

***

"That movie was so good," Erika said after we had arrived at Diary Queen. "I know I've seen it like every year since I was three, but I always cry at the ending."

"You cry at beer commercials," Rick teased her.

"I do not," she slapped his arm, gently. "I mean, this movie just shows how good and kind people can be when you're in trouble and need help. That even though you might go through tough times, life is worth living because you have friends around."

"I guess that's the basic point of the movie, never give up hope, there will be a brighter tomorrow," Luke Reasoned. "But I also got out of it that every time a bell rings, an angel gets its wings."

"That reminds me," Rick said. "I think I'll get some onion rings."

"Hi Rick," We all looked up at the same time and standing by our table with a bright smile, jeans, and t-shirt, was Sam. "How's it going?"

"Oh, pretty good. You remember Luke?"

"Oh yeah. Hi. Long time."

"Yup," Luke drawled. "Been in Oklahoma for the past three years."

"Cool," he looked at me for the first time and stuck his hand out, which I took, shaking it briskly.

"Oh, that there is Phillip," Rick introduced us. "He was with me at the gas station the other day. He's Hank's nephew and is staying there for a while. And of course, you know Erika."

"So, Sam, what brings you here today?" Erika asked.

"An appetite," Sam had a 'duh' expression on his cute face. "Just

64

got off work and thought I'd get something quick to eat. What have you all been up to today?"

"We just came from the Old Majestic Theater," Erika answered.

"So, um..." Rick stammered. "You want to join us or something?"

"Nah, that's okay. I was just going to get takeout and head home. Y'all have a pleasant evening." He left to go order his food. Rick fidgeted in his seat as Luke watched him leave.

All the soda I drank at the theater suddenly had gotten to me as I found myself squirming in my chair.

"Excuse me, but where's the rest room?" I ask no one in particular.

"It's right through there," Luke pointed in the direction in the back of the restaurant.

"Thanks. I'll be right back. Don't touch my fries," I warned Erika.

"I ain't making no promises," she shot back.

Once in the restroom I drained my bladder, much to my relief. No one else was in there, so I whistled a Christmas tune, Jingle Bells. The door opened and closed, and a guy came up to the urinal just as I was finishing. I glanced over to see Sam standing beside me. He wasn't using the urinal, he just stared at me for a moment until I met his eyes.

"Hey," he said.

"Hey." I went over to the sink to wash my hands, he followed.

"Just waiting on my order. Thought maybe I would come in here and mess around a bit."

"What did you have in mind?" I asked as I grabbed hold a paper towel and dried my hands.

"It seems Rick is taken. When Luke is around, there is no other for him. He is pretty faithful that way. He never cheats."

"Good to know," I said, tossing the towel in the trash bin.

He leaned in close and his mouth touched my ear, tickling it.

"I saw you the other day watching us. I know you liked what you saw. Maybe we can do something real quick before I get my order."

"Um...they might wonder where I am," I said, breathing hard.

He guided me backwards to the back of the restroom, my back against the wall, he kissed me softly.

"Let them wonder."

He dropped his jeans, revealing a hard-seven-inch cut dick and blond pubes surrounding it. With large, juicy balls dangled underneath.

"Suck it," he whispered.

I went down on my knees to eye level with his beautiful cock. I wrapped my lips around the head and slowly sunk more of the shaft into my mouth. While his cock disappeared inside the warm cavern, I gently rolled his balls in my hand. Looking up at him, I saw his head was thrown back and eyes closed. He moaned and writhed above me as I sucked his dick and played with his balls.

I moved back up to the head and licked it and the piss slit and under the ridge.

"Oh yeah," he moaned. "Here," he pulled me up and pushed me inside a stall, closing and locking it. "More privacy," he said as he sunk to his knees and unzipped my fly, pulling my hard and straining dick out. It was already dripping with pre-cum, he licked it off the tip of my cock head, then swallowed my whole dick inside his wet hot mouth.

"Oh, my God," I gasped. His thick puffy lips wrapped tightly around the shaft, he moved from the base back to the head and then back again. Going faster with each stroke. "Fuck," I said. I couldn't help myself. I hardly ever curse, but the pleasure was immense. It brought memories of when Rick first sucked me, and I wished it was him on his knees now. But Sam wasn't a bad replacement as he had mad skills.

"If you keep that up, I'm gonna cum soon," I warned."

He released my dripping, saliva-soaked cock and slowly rose, planting kisses on my stomach and chest on his way to my mouth where he landed a passionate toe curling kiss.

"We gotta make this quick," he said. "But I want to cum first. On your knees, now," he ordered.

I obeyed and placed his hard cock in my hungry mouth and sucked him. My head bobbed on his cock, sucking and licking. My hand fondled his large balls.

He started to face fuck me. I could sense he was close. I could feel his cock pulse as he shot a powerful load down my mouth. I kept sucking and swallowing. He kept thrusting and moaning. I pulled away from his cock, the last drop of cum dangled from the tip. I licked it off him and he shuddered.

"That was awesome," he said with a wide grin. I noticed for the first time he had dimples, giving him a charm I was sure Rick adored. "Now, your turn."

Sam took my dick in hand and jacked it a few times, rubbing his thumb over the sensitive head. Then he knelt and once again went down on my cock, slurping and licking. My head spun with the pleasure of his blowjob and I almost lost my balance. I had to spread my arms out to the walls on either side of me. He went at me like a hungry wolf, devouring my cock and lapping at my balls.

I felt the fire deep inside my loins, a burning desire for release. The cum boiled within me and was about to shatter my urethra and come forth through blasts of euphoria.

"Ah, ah, ah," words were escaping me, I had no cognizance of verbal intelligence. "Uh...ooh!" I cried out at last. My cum filled his mouth as he continued to suck. Some of it dribbled down his chin, most he swallowed.

He backed away and wiped his face with his sleeve.

"Wow, that was awesome," he said. "Well, I gotta dash." He was gone in a flash. I stood there still bracing the stall walls. My dick hung out from my fly. Dripping were the remnants of my seed.

I realized I had been fantasizing about Rick while Sam blew me. In my fevered mind, it was Rick on his knees. It was Rick who made me cum. I knew it was hopeless. I feared that every man I might be with in my life would be a stand in for Rick. Maybe some day I would get over him, like I had gotten over Barry. I hadn't even thought of Barry for a while now, it was as if he no longer existed. Somehow, I thought it might be harder to forget about Rick. He would stay with me forever. Forever in my heart.

"What took you so long?" Erika asked, popping one of my fries in her mouth.

"I drank a lot of soda," was my only explanation, which they seemed to except, for now.

Chapter Nine

"You ready for your hot date tonight?" Erika poked her head in my bedroom door as I pulled a red Christmas shirt over my head. The shirt had Rudolph on the front, complete with a shiny red nose that blinks. Erika smirked at me when she saw it.

"It's not a date," I reminded her.

"Sure," she came in and plopped on my bed. "Whatever."

"Make yourself at home, why don't you."

"Always do," she responded. "I think you will have lots of fun, even if it's not a date. There are a lot of great guys in town. A lot of gay, single guys," she emphasized.

"I'm sure there are. Randy and Seth seem like great guys."

"They're a couple, you know," she revealed.

"Really?"

"Yeah. They have an open relationship, or so I've heard. Maybe they want a threesome with you."

"Um...well...I don't know," I stammered, bowing my red face down, staring at the floor.

"Hey, you might have come here a virgin, but I know you have been having lots of sex since you've been here. Don't think I don't know what you and Sam were doing in the restroom at DQ."

My head shot up and I looked at her in amazement. Did she have a crystal ball?

"Girl, how do you know everything?" I asked.

"I see all. I know all," she said, cryptically raising her eyebrows up and down. "I just happened to look up and saw Sam sneaking off to the restroom. I only guessed the rest." She pulled a leg up on the bed under her. "So, what's with the shirt?"

I looked down at Rudolph.

"It's Christmas."

"I know that, but don't you want to wear something nicer for your date?"

"It's not a date," I said for the umpteenth time.

"Okay, okay, so it's not a date."

"My mom got this for me last Christmas so thought I'd wear it at least once."

"Why not wait until Christmas day to wear it, then?"

"I'm wearing a snowman one that day," I smiled.

Three quick knocks at my bedroom door alerted us to someone's presence. Rick stood outside the doorway.

"Decent?" He asked, peering in.

"As if you would care," Erika snidely said.

"Uh, yeah," I said, checking to make sure my fly was zipped up.

"Okay good. They're here. They just pulled up. So... ready to go?"

"Yeah. Ready as I'll ever be." I said, yet not feeling nearly as ready for a night out.

"Good," he leaned into the room, as if trying to think of something he had forgotten. "Um...have fun tonight." My stomach knotted up as he left the room.

"Gosh, he's so gorgeous," I told Erika. "If I only had one Christmas wish...I'll...," I stopped there, unable to finish that sentence.

"You'll wish for Rick naked with a big red bow tied around his neck and you'll be the happiest boy in the world," Erika finished for me. She really did know everything. "In lieu of that," she got off the bed and gave me a peck on the cheek. "Try to have fun tonight. It will cheer you up."

***

It was karaoke night which Seth and Randy had neglected to tell me. They tried their best to talk
me into doing a song but I told them no, I don't sing. However, every fives minutes they would ask again, and I told them no thank you. A cute blond guy on stage by the name of Ray performed a stunning rendition of Blue Christmas. He wiggled his hips some as music moved him and he sang with a definitive country twang.

"He ain't half bad," Seth said, sipping his beer.

"Yup," Randy agreed. "Ray up there can really carry a tune. I bet you can too, Phillip."

Was the five minutes up already? I wondered.

"Look guys, I appreciate your confidence in me, but I'm not a singer. I would make a fool out of myself if I got up there."

"Look," Randy started. "Ray is one of the few guys here who can sing, the rest of 'em can't sing worth shit. So, no one ain't gonna make fun of you just cause your voice sounds like a sick seal. We ain't American Idol here you know."

"Why don't you take a sip of my beer," Seth suggested. "It might help loosen you up some."

"I'm not sure guys," I looked at them both with yearning eyes. I really wanted to taste it to see what it would be like but didn't know if I should.

"Go on," Randy encouraged. "What could it hurt, just one sip."

Seth handed me his glass of beer and I tentatively took a sip. I decided I liked the taste, a little bitter, but not too bad. I had another sip before anyone could stop me, then handed the glass back to Seth.

"No, you drink the rest of it, I'll get another."

"But...," I was about to protest when Seth waved me off and summoned a server to our table to order another beer.

I finished off the beer that Seth gave me in no time. He only took a few sips out of his fresh beer, when he turned to me and said: "I ain't that thirsty anyhow so why don't you finish this one up," then pushed the glass of beer towards me. Without thinking, I took it and gulped it down.

Randy had ordered another beer for himself but said he couldn't finish it, so he pushed his glass towards me, and I finished it off for him, it was more than halfway full.

"Gee guys, you are the best," I squeezed both of their arms. "You're both so muscular and sexy," they were wearing plaid shirts, Seth's was blue and Randy's was red. I moved my hand up and down their arms, feeling their muscles. "And both of you have very nice asses," I hiccupped.

"I think he had enough," Seth said.

"Yup," Randy concurred.

"I think I'm gonna sing now," I said giddily. "I feel like singing."

"Uh...do you think that's a good idea?" Seth said.

"Well, you're the one who wanted me to, now I'm ready," I stood up wobbly.

"But," Randy pushed me back into my chair. "You're inebriated."

I stared out him like he was a creature from outer space.

"Don't even know what that means," in my mind I was saying everything right, but the reality was, I slurred my words together and it came out more as "donsh knos wheyts thetas meanshes."

"It means, you have had one two many," Seth clarified.

"No!" I slapped the table. "I only had half of yours," I pointed to Seth. "And half of yours," I pointed to Randy. "And half of yours," I pointed to Seth again. "So, you see gentlemen, I'm perfectly able to go up there and sing without looking like an idiot."

I got up to on the stage before they could stop me and took the mic from some poor old slob who was singing White Christmas, he was just singing 'May all your Christmas's be..." when I interrupted him and he said "Fuck you." *Funny, I don't remember that in the lyrics,* I thought.

For some reason, though it was a blur, I noticed Randy and Seth with their faces buried in their hands. They looked embarrassed.

"Okay," I said, looking out over the stunned crowd. "I'm gonna sing a song in honor of Rudolph," I started getting emotional thinking of poor Rudolph. "They wouldn't let him play any reindeer games," I sobbed. "Not until he saved Christmas one year...bunch of pricks." I looked heavenward, "so this song is for you Rudolph, you sweet red nosed deer."

I started to sing and couldn't remember all the words, so I made some up. I was getting hot and for some reason thought it would be best if I stripped out of my shirt. I sang and swirled around shaking my hips and got hotter, so I continued to strip. When I got down to my underwear, Randy and Seth came up and carried me off stage over one of their shoulders.

"Thank you very much," I said, as we passed people. I must have been terrible, yet as we were going into the back room, I heard applause, it could have been because they were glad I was finally off the stage.

They placed me on a pool table, my legs splayed out, my crotch growing larger. I was getting horny being manhandled by two gorgeous cowboys.

"Is he alright?" The cutie who sang earlier, Ray, asked as he came into the back room.

"I think he'll be fine. Just drank a little much."

"Hey, are we gonna have sex?" I asked, sticking my hand in my underwear and squeezing my dick.

"Hell yeah!" Ray seemed up for it as he started to unbutton his shirt.

"I don't think that's a good idea," Randy said. "You're a little drunk."

"I know what I want and I want to have sex. I'm horny as hell," I slipped off my underwear and my dick popped out and stuck straight up.

All three of them looked at it like it was their last meal.

"Well, we don't want to disappoint him," Seth said.

"I think you're right, Seth," Randy said.

"Just don't stick anything in my butt," I warned. "I'm saving that for Rick," I giggled. "Rick, I wish he was here. He's loads of fun."

"I'm sure he is," Randy said as he slipped my dick into his mouth and started sucking me.

"Oh God!" I grabbed hold of Randy's bobbing head. "You suck good."

Seth and Ray were removing their clothes quickly.

"What if someone comes in?" Ray worried.

"I wouldn't worry too much about that," Seth said. "They usually close this part of the bar down during karaoke night and if someone happens to come in, maybe they will join us."

Randy got off my dick and pointed it at Seth who immediately went down on it while Randy began to strip.

"Ah, God! There's a lot of good suckers in this town." I wasn't aware of how that sounded, but in my mind at the time, it sounded logical.

"Me next," Ray said and sunk down on my wet cock after Seth had left it.

Seth immediately went to my balls and started sucking and nibbling. Randy wasn't to be left out as he climbed on the pool table and dangled his large uncut dick in my face. I stuck my tongue out and lapped at it. He humped my face rubbing his slick cock over my lips as he stretched himself out over my prone body and helped Ray with my cock, taking turns sucking and licking and slurping on it.

Ray didn't mind sharing my dick with Randy as it gave him the opportunity to kiss him when their lips met at the tip of my dick. Seth pulled up from my balls and made it a three-way kiss fest. All three men licked up and down my shaft, meeting at the head to kiss. Then one of them would go down and suck for a few seconds, followed by one of the others.

My mouth was full of Randy's dick. He pumped it in and out. My hand moved around to his firm ass and I found his hole. Gently poking it with a finger until it opened up for me and allowed me entry. He moaned over my dick, sending vibrations through my aching body.

I slipped his dick out of my mouth and swallowed his balls, sucking on them while I finger fucked him.

"Oh God!" He said when he had lifted off my cock. He sat up, disconnecting my mouth from his balls and my finger from his hole.

Seth took over sucking while Randy sat on my face, his hole over my mouth. I licked and poked it with my tongue. With Randy over my face I couldn't see who was sucking me, but my dick was being sucked as well as my balls. Then I felt two tongues licking my shaft up and down. My head was spinning with man sex.

"God, I gotta have your dick in me," Randy said lifting off my face suddenly. He retrieved his discarded jeans and pulled out a packet of condoms and a small bottle of lube. "I always come prepared," he said with a grin.

Seth and Ray stopped sucking me and helped to put the condom on my dick and to slick it up with lube. They put a generous amount of lube in Randy's hole as well.

Soon, Randy stood over me on the table and lowered himself, spreading his cheeks, while Seth held my dick and guided it in Randy's hole. Randy sunk down further until my whole dick was inside him. He grunted and squirmed on it. He sat there for a little while getting used to it.

"Okay, we can make this more interesting," Randy said. He had Seth get another condom and he put it on his cock and had Seth spread it with lube. He had Seth get up and sit on his cock. He told Ray to get up over my face and to place his cock on my mouth and to have his mouth on Seth's cock.

Randy to bounced on my cock. Seth stayed still and allowed Randy to fuck himself up into his ass as he bounced on me. In the meanwhile, I had Ray's cock in my mouth as he was fucking my face while he had Seth's cock in his mouth as Seth fucked into his mouth while Randy bounced away.

It didn't take too long for me to cum. I felt it bubbling up, ready to squirt out inside the condom. I let out a garbled scream since I had Ray's cock in my mouth. My cum filled the condom in Randy's ass to overflowing. This set Randy off and he tightened his hole around my shaft as he shot his load in Seth's ass.

Since Randy didn't stop bouncing once I had cum and with the added friction of his hole tightening, I came again. I nearly passed out from the extreme pleasure, though I managed to keep my consciousness during the intense sensations I felt through my whole body.

Seth soon filled Ray's mouth with his cum and screamed obscenities as he released his load, some of which dripped down onto my stomach.

Ray got up, turned around, sat down on my chest, his dripping cock pointed towards me. I grasped him with my hand and jerked him off fast.

"I'm cumming," he said, breathlessly. His cum soon flew out of his dickhead and over my head, splattering all over the floor beyond. "God. That was the best cum I ever had."

I suddenly felt the room spinning, it seemed like I was on a merry-go-round which kept going faster and faster. Soon, there was nothing but blackness.

Chapter Ten

I awoke with a warm body beside me, and an arm draped over my waist. Soft breathing tickled my ear. The fuzzy events of the night before came more into focus as daylight began to stream into my room. I didn't know how I got here or what happened after I had passed out, but I remembered the sex. And the singing...

"Oh God," I groaned.

I needed to tell Randy or Seth or whoever was beside me he needed to leave. I lifted the limp arm off me and groggily sat up. My head ached, so I sat on the edge of the bed with my hands cradling my head.

I heard movement behind me and a yawn.

"How you feel?"

I spun around when I heard his voice, causing a dizzy spell. I tried to keep a grip but stumbled to the floor. He looked down at me, trying to suppress a laugh.

It was Rick.

"You okay there, Buddy?"

"Sure," I said, unsure whether I was dreaming somehow, or maybe last night had been a dream. "What...what are you.," I noticed I was in my undies, so I pulled the blanket off the bed to cover up, revealing he also had only undies on, and morning wood by the looks of it.

"To answer your question, I was outside on the porch when Randy and Seth brought you home. I saw you were out of it, so I helped you up here to your room."

"Did you have to spend the night here?" I asked.

"Thought I'd stay in case you puked or something."

"Ah, okay."

"So, I take it you had a good time last night?"

"Uh...I guess so."

"Good. I'll get you some aspirin and water, I'm sure you must have a headache."

"Yeah, thanks." In truth, the adrenalin from finding him in my bed had gotten rid the worst of it.

When I had pulled myself together, I went down for breakfast. Uncle Hank said he wanted me to go with Jake and help him mend a fence on the south side of the ranch after I had eaten.

There always seemed to be some fence in need of mending around these parts.

Jake was a quiet and an unassuming man. He worked hard and was easy going. He showed me what to do and helped me out a lot when I needed it. The sun heated our bodies as we worked, and Jake took his hat off, wiping sweat from his forehead.

"You hungry?" He asked, sitting down on a tree stump.

"Yes!" I said. I was starved even after a big breakfast. Hard work really did make me get a big appetite.

"I asked Rosa to pack us some lunch so we can eat it right here. There's a pond just up that path that I think would make a nice eating spot."

"Sounds good," I said.

Watching Jake go up to the truck to get the packed lunch and seeing his ass so firm and shapely in his tight jeans really made me hungry for something more. But Uncle Hank had said Jake was straight. I didn't expect anything to happen, but a boy can dream.

"This way," Jake said as he led me down the path. A short while later we were at a small pond. There were a few small trees around it and the water looked so refreshing to my dry mouth.

"This here is a good spot," he said as he laid out the blanket he had brought and set the food down. I could smell the fried chicken even before he took it out of the basket.

"This is nice, Jake," I told him. "It's really pretty here."

"I figured you would like it," Jake said as he bit into a chicken leg. "Some of the guys like to swim in that pond. A lot of times they would go skinny dipping."

"Really?"

"Yup. It's real private here, miles away from anything. We got mountains surrounding us, we got some trees," he gestured around the pretty scenery.

"Have you ever gone skinny dipping, Jake?" I asked, feeling silly for having brought it up.

"Nope. But it's such a warm day today and I've been working hard, I just might. Just to cool off, of course. You wouldn't mind, would you?"

"Oh, of course I wouldn't mind. I would love to...I mean; it would be okay." Oops, I was about to tell him I wanted to see his cock.

"So, did you have a good time last night? I noticed the state you were in when they dropped you off while I was on the porch with Rick, shooting the breeze."

"Uh...yeah. I had a pretty good time."

"You should have seen the state Rick was in, chewing them out for getting you drunk."

"He did. He didn't say anything about that this...," I trailed off not sure if I should finish that sentence and took a sip from a bottle of coke Jake had brought.

"Hey, I know he spent the night with you," he said. "I helped him tuck you in. He wanted to stay in case you needed something in the night."

"Like a bucket?" I surmised.

"Yup," Jake took a long sip of his coke, his Adam's apple bobbed as he swallowed the cool liquid down his throat.

Someone came up from behind and grabbed me.

"Hey," I said, struggling. When I glanced back, Rick stood there with his arms around my mid-section laughing his ass off. Luke was beside him, also with a big goofy grin on his handsome face. "What's the big idea?"

"Just keeping you on your toes," Rick said. "You never know what's lurking in the shadows," he did a scary laugh.

I noticed they didn't try that with Jake. He was big and strong and probably would have pummeled them into the ground. Or maybe not since Jake is a gentle, easy going guy.

"What are y'all doing here?" Jake asked.

"Just thought we'd go for a quick swim," Luke said. "We parked our horses over yonder," he pointed in the direction where I could see the horses, including blaze, standing. "So, you wouldn't hear us when we snuck up."

"Worked like a charm," I said under my breath.

"We were just thinking we might go for a swim too," Jake said.

"Really?" Rick said. "Cool."

Both Luke and Rick started to strip. I've seen Rick naked, but now I had the opportunity to see Luke. When he got down to his underwear, I could see what a beautiful man Luke was, and felt even more jealous that I could never compete with a man like him. His dick was cut and six inches, soft. Thick blond pubic hair appeared above his dick and when he turned and ran into the pond, I had to catch my breath. His ass was a completely tanned tight orbs of splendor.

"Why don't y'all finish eating after a dip in the pond," Rick advised, his big, beautiful dick swinging casually between his legs just inches from my face. He raced to the pond and did a cannon ball, making a big splash. "Come in. The water's great," he backstroked.

"Well, what the hell," Jake said and stripped naked too. I soon discovered he wasn't wearing underwear as he slid his jeans down and his big black uncut dick came into view. A trail of hair led from his belly button to his thick bush of pubic hair. His legs were well muscled and strong. He had a thin waist and wide shoulders. He was sexy and my dick immediately sprang up in the confines of my own jeans.

"Come on, Phillip. How 'bout we join them," Jake said.

"I will in a minute," I said, willing my erection to go down.

"Suit yourself," he said and ran into the pond. His ass a thing of pure beauty and I thought to myself that it's too bad he's straight.

After a couple of minutes my dick went soft and thought it would be safe to strip and join in the fun. They were splashing and seemed to be having a good time. Someone whistled as I took off my underwear. I wasn't sure why, but my skin felt warm with yet another blush. I sped into the pond and dove in, bumping into Rick. He groped my dick and balls and I was in danger of being erect again. He began jacking me.

"Fancy meeting you here," he said with a grin.

"What are you doing?" I whispered, shocked by his overtures.

"What does it look like?" He whispered back.

"Rick, not here," I begged, looking over my shoulders to see if the others had noticed Rick making a move on me.

"Then where, if not here?" He countered.

"Hey guys," Luke swam quickly by our sides. "What are you two doing over here?"

"Just jacking his dick," Rick casually said. My face grew redder. I couldn't believe he admitted it to his lover.

"Really?" Luke's hand went underwater and felt Rick's hand and then my dick. He took over jacking from Rick whose hand went to my rear and felt through my crack.

"Hey guys. What's up over there?" Jake called from across the pond.

"If you don't want to witness gay sex, Jake, then you best close your eyes," Rick called over to him. I couldn't see Jake's expression, so I had no idea how he felt about what Rick had said. But I thought Rick might just be kidding. He couldn't possibly have sex with me out here in the open with his boyfriend and Jake around.

Rick picked me up and carried me to shore. My shaking body dripping wet and red all over from embarrassment. My dick stuck straight out, begging for attention and it looked as though Rick was about to give it some.

Luke followed us out and knelt on the blanket as Rick laid me out. I could see Jake walking to the shore with a perplexed yet intrigued expression. To my astonishment, it wasn't Rick who went down on me but Luke. He took my dick into his mouth without hesitation.

"Oh God!" It was a little embarrassing doing this in front of Jake. He was a nice man and very straight. I didn't know how he would take seeing gay sex up close like this. Luke was a good cocksucker. He sucked up and down for a few minutes and then Rick took over. They were giving me tingles all over. And the juices in my balls were flowing and quivering for sweet release. "Oh! This is...ah" I could hardly speak. The feelings were so great. They took turns sucking me hard and fast, one after the other, switching off. I squirmed under their ministrations and was about to boil over. "Guys! I'm gonna! Oh God!" My dick was in Luke's mouth when my first shot blasted out. They took turns taking my load, switching from Luke's mouth to Rick's until my dick was spent and went soft again. "Oh wow! uh...God!"

"Oh man! That was hot," Jake stood near us, his cock hard as he jacked it.

"Well, bring that cock over here and we'll give it the same treatment," Luke suggested.

"I don't know guys. I mean...," Jake trailed off as though he might be considering it.

"What do you have to lose, Jake?" Rick said. "A really hot blow job from three awesome guys would blow your mind in more ways than one," Rick teased, and licked my cock one last time, causing me to whimper.

"Gee, I'm so horny right now. It's been a while since my girl and I... oh, what the hell. As you said, what do I have to lose?"

"Exactly," Luke agreed. "Except maybe a large load of cum," he smiled.

"Lie down here, beside Phillip," Rick said.

Jake did as he was told. His cock, which seemed to be at least eleven inches was sticking straight up into the air. Luke and Rick didn't waste much time and practically bumped their heads together diving for his meaty cock. They rubbed their mouths on either side of the huge cock and Luke plunged down and swallowed half of Jake's cock in one go.

"Oh wow! Man! That's...aw...God!" Jake was moaning. "I ain't never had a blow job before...and this.... oh wow...this is so great."

"Your girl never gave you a blow job?" Rick asked, perplexed.

"Nope. She never wanted it in her mouth. And she didn't even like me fucking her much...oh God...because she said it was too big and it hurt her."

"Well, you need to find yourself another woman, Jake. Lots of women would love a cock this big, I'm sure. Until then, you can count on us gay boys to take care of your needs," Rick assured him. With that, Rick moved down and gently bumped Luke out of the way and went down on Jake's throbbing spit covered black cock. And he went all the way down to Jake's curly black pubes.

"Oh God!" He screamed. "You're able to take the whole thing? God! Why have I never done this before?"

They had him thrashing and swearing and shaking as they gave him the same treatment they had given me. Jake looked at me. I hadn't joined in yet, but the way Jake had gotten into gay sex had begun to make my cock hard again. Jake motioned for me to come over to him.

"I don't know if I will be any good at it or if I would like it," Jake told me, "but I want to try sucking cock. Put it in my mouth and fuck my face," he said. The expression on my face must have shown shock or bewilderment, because Jake then said, "It's alright, man. I won't bite it, I promise."

I straddled his face and pointed my once again hard dick to his mouth and plunged in. His tongue immediately swirled around my shaft. The warmth and wetness of his mouth felt good on my cock. I began to thrust in and out, fucking his face. The sensation was amazing. For a beginner, he was able to take it like a pro.

Now that I was in on the action, I wanted a taste of his dick too, and while I fucked his face, I leaned in enough to suck his dick. Both Luke and Rick held it for me and I sucked on the head and down a couple of inches. His cock throbbed in my mouth and his pre-cum leaked out of his shaft like a faucet.

Rick lifted my face from Jake's dick and kissed me on the lips. As we made out Luke went back to work on Jake's cock. I was fucking my cock in and out of Jake's mouth and felt I was on the verge of my explosion. I didn't think Jake would want me to cum inside his mouth, so I broke off the kiss with Rick to warn him.

I pulled out and sat on Jake's chest. Jake jacked me as Rick and I resumed our make out session. Rick's hand moved down my body and joined Jake's hand in helping me cum while playing with my balls.

"Oh God!" I moaned into Rick's mouth My hips lifted off Jake's chest and cum shot out of my dickhead over Jake's and Rick's hands and into the air, onto Jake's chin, it splattered everywhere. Rick broke our kiss and leaned down to take my still spurting cock in his mouth. "Oh God!" My dick was becoming sensitive to the touch and I squirmed around as Rick tried to lap up the rest of my oozing cum.

We moved down to Luke and helped with Jake's orgasm. As Luke sucked, Rick and I jacked the huge cock in synchronized sexual heat, Rick's hand under mine, twisting and jacking into Luke's watering mouth. We jacked faster and harder while Luke took as much of the cock as he could. We had Jake thrashing and screaming, his body tensed, his legs stiffened.

"Oh God! I'm gonna cum! Oh man! Yes! Yes! Yes! Aw! God yes! Ooh! Uh...uh!" His butt left the ground as his cum shot from his dick into Luke's mouth. Luke managed to swallow all of it, much to Jake's amazement.

When he finally came down from his high, he gathered up his clothes and quickly dressed. He looked as though he had just run a marathon. "That was great, guys. I can't believe I did that though," he chuckled, as he zipped his jeans up.

"Would you be willing to do it again sometime?" Luke asked, hopefully.

Jake thought for a moment.

"Probably. It was really something else. Didn't expect to enjoy it as much as I did. Man, my cock is still tingling," he chuckled.

"Well, glad we could be of service," Rick said, with a sexy half smile.

"Think I'm gonna go back and get some more work done," Jake said. "You stay here for a while, Phillip. Have some more lunch. See you guys later," Jake walked back in the direction we had come from.

"Can't believe he did that, sucked your dick," Rick said to me. "Guess he was so horny he forgot he was straight."

Chapter Eleven

After Jake had left, the three of us just sat and ate lunch and talked. It was a nice breezy day. There were blue skies and fluffy white clouds scattered around taking on various shapes. We were looking at them trying to make a guess at what we thought they looked like. Luke said he was sure there was a pig flying up there somewhere, but Rick and I couldn't see it. Rick could have sworn he saw a large dick and balls floating in the sky, his mind still very much on sex. I thought it was more of a baseball bat with two hands gripping it.

"You think we freaked Jake out?" Luke asked suddenly.

We were deep in thought. I thought about how fun it was to do those things with Jake. He was awesome and really seemed to enjoy it. But he did flee right after he came.

"Well," Rick said, "he did like it. You can tell these things about a person. He could be a little freaked that he did it, but I have a feeling he might have been thinking about it for a spell now. Like something he wanted to do, at least to try it, but was afraid to."

"Makes sense," I said. "Maybe I should get back to work." I didn't want to be known as a slacker and there was still work to be done.

"Not so fast mister," Rick stopped me from getting dressed as he hopped up from his sitting spot and grabbed me. "I ain't finished with you yet," he said with a smirk. "And you still need to be punished for getting drunk last night."

"W-what do you mean?" I asked, his hand firmly held my arm as his steely gaze mesmerized me into submission.

"I mean," he said as he gently pushed me back down on the blanket, "I'm still horny."

Rick had the look of a hungry wolf capturing his prey. He was going to devour me and leave me quivering upon the brink of sexual anguish.

Luke crawled over to us. He had the same look of lust filling his sparkling blue eyes. His golden hair whipped around his face as the warm Texas wind caressed his handsome face.

"I want to fuck you," Rick growled. "I want to fuck you hard."

I was stunned so said nothing. He was so animalistic, and it seemed Luke was there for whatever ride I was about to go on.

Rick rubbed his dick along my ass crack, kissing me hard on the lips. Luke slipped his hand between me and Rick finding my dick and caressed it gently. His fingers ran the length of my dick, tickling the sensitive skin.

"Do you want to be fucked by a rugged cowboy?" Rick asked, eyes blazing with red-hot embers of lust.

"Oh yes!" I said, my heart fiercely beating in my chest. He made me so horny, my dick was hard once again, even though I had already cum twice.

As Rick slid down my body towards my spread legs, Luke had more room now to really wrap his fingers around my dick to jack me. He licked his pointed tipped tongue at the head as he coaxed pre-cum out through the piss slit.

Luke caressed my thighs and reached my balls, which he tenderly cupped.

"Mmm," I moaned with delight, shaking slightly.

Rick roughly pushed a finger into my hole, I screamed with sudden pain. I've never been fucked but was willing to give up my complete virginity to this cowboy whom I secretly loved but feared I could never fully have. Sam's words rung in my ears. 'Rick never cheats.' And yet, he here was now, doing things with me and Jake. His lover by his side. Was this only a one-time thing? Something that may never occur again. It broke my heart to think about, so I pushed it aside for now and enjoyed the things they were doing to my body.

Rick wiggled his finger around while I squirmed and moaned. Luke sucked in the head of my dick into his mouth. It was a mixture of pain and pleasure. It felt weird but at the same time, wonderful. Luke went down on my cock all the way to my bush. He squeezed my balls, not hard, yet not gentle. They wanted to play rough and I was determined to take what they gave me. I whimpered but tried not to cry out too much, even when Rick added another finger to my hole.

"I'm gonna fuck you until you see stars," he said in his sexy baritone voice as he finger fucked me with two fingers, pushing in and out. "And you're gonna love it," he said as a statement of truth. He added a third finger, stretching my hole out, I wasn't sure it would accommodate his huge dick, but I was willing to give it a try. Just to feel him inside me. "Luke," he said, and Luke lifted his head from my dripping cock. "Suck on my dick for a while, I'm gonna eat his ass out then he will be ready to go."

Luke moved down to Rick's dick as Rick buried his head in my ass. His tongue entered my hole, which was soothing compared to his rough fingers. Luke went to town on Rick's dick, bobbing his head fast on the big tool, while Rick slobbered all over my ass. Licking and spitting in my hole, he would occasionally lick up to my taint and onto my balls and slipped them into his mouth and sucked and rolled them around. Then he moved up to my throbbing dick and swallowed it down his gullet and sucked a few strokes on it and then went back down to my ass.

"Easy there, Luke," Rick pulled his dick from Luke's pre-cum and saliva-soaked mouth. "Don't want to cum before I get the chance to fuck. Get some lube," he told him.

Luke went to fetch Rick's jeans and pulled out a small bottle of lube. These guys came prepared, I thought. Rick squirted some on his hand and began fingering me again while Luke applied some of the lube to Rick's big fat dick. Rick's cock looked bigger and fatter than ever before and I wondered how that thing was going to fit inside me. My hole clenched around his finger as I thought about it.

Rick pointed his dick at my hole, rubbing the head on it, swirling around the pucker, then he pushed in and I screamed out. He stopped, letting me get used to it. Only the head was in so far and it was painful for me. He pushed in a little more and then a little more.

"God, your tight," he said. "Feels really good around my big fat dick."

I kept trying to remember to breath, trying to relax, wanting this no matter the pain. I have heard it will turn to pleasure, though now I was in agony. Rick was so big and I had never been fucked before. It was like he was splitting me in two.

Perhaps sensing my distress, Luke came over and started sucking my dick again, trying to lessen the feel of a thick cock inside such a tight space. Luke's mouth felt good and I began to relax a little. My legs wrapped around Rick's back, and he pushed in further.

After a few minutes, he was finally all the way in.

"Hit rock bottom," he said with a sexy grin.

Rick fucked me slowly at first. In and out, in and out. Luke sucked my cock like a mad man. My moans echoed through the hills. We were lucky we were far away from other people. Tucked in our own little private oasis.

Eventually, the pain had gone away and replaced with pleasure. My insides were still on fire, but the pleasure button had been found.

"Oh God!" I moaned.

"Oh yes!" Rick shouted. His own pleasure in fucking me written all over his handsome, chiseled face.

Luke abandoned my cock and moved up to my face, He straddled me. Pointing his cock to my mouth, which I gladly took.

Rick, seeing the ass in front of his face, leaned up to lick Luke's ass crack. He grabbed the ass cheeks and spread them, holding onto them as he fucked me. Rick licked deeper within Luke's secret spot, finding his hole, and sending his tongue down the chute.

We continued this way for several minutes, each of us writhing and grinding into each other. When suddenly, Rick pulled out of me, my hole gaping and dripping with lube. I felt empty without him in me.

"Okay, Luke, get in front of Phillip. Phillip, stick your dick in Luke's ass, fuck him good."

I did as he said and pushed my dick inside Luke.

"Oh, yeah!" Luke moaned. "Feels good."

Luke was tight but my cock went in easily. I slid it back and forth a few times. Rick held me from behind and pushed his own cock back inside of me. When Rick stabbed me with his dick it pushed me further into Luke, Luke moaned and wiggled his ass, wanting more. Rick and I moved out and then back in. We built up a rhythm and moved with each other. When I pulled out, he pulled out, and we both slammed back in. We went faster and harder with every passing minute. My body ached with the need of sexual release as I knew the end was near. Coming upon the Promised Land.

The two golden globes of Luke's ass jiggled as I fucked him. His balls slapped against thighs; his dick bounced underneath him. I reach around and jacked his cock. Sliding my hand from base to head, I jacked him fast and hard, as I fucked him with furious strokes. Rick fucked me roughly now that I'm open enough. He stroked my prostate with the head of his dick as he reached to the most inner parts of my being.

We were three men fucking together, thrusting, sweating, moaning under the hot Texas sun. The sound of slapping flesh, thrashing on a blanket in the dust, was all that could be heard as we shut out the whole world, and only knew in that moment, three naked bodies begging for the release they have been craving. And they won't be denied that sweet release.

"Oh! Oh! Oh!" Luke splattered his cum over my jacking hand and down on the blanket. "God! Yes!" He sighed a heavy breath.

"Oh God! I'm gonna cum," My cum shot out just as I pulled out. Rick quickly wrapped his hand around my shaft and jacked me, squeezing out load after load of hot semen across Luke's ass. Rick's hand was getting wet and sticky with my cum. He milked out the last drop from my dickhead and wiped his cum drenched hand on my heaving stomach.

Rick continued to fuck me and soon was swearing and hollering.

"Cumming!" He yelled out at the top of his lungs. I could feel his cum shooting out of his dick and into my ass. Filling me with his juices. "Oh wow!" He pulled out and sat back on his hunches. He looked sexy with his dripping cock, still throbbing, his balls hanging low, his knees splayed out wide as he leaned back. His dick pointed up towards his face. His stomach moved up and down with his heavy breathing. "That was the best fuck I had in a long time," he sighed with relief.

I knew I should be getting back to work. I didn't want to disappoint my uncle.

"I better get going," I said as I collected my clothes. "Still have some work for today."

"Yeah, us too," Luke said. "This was really fun though. We should do it again soon."

"Yeah, maybe," Rick said as he too gathered up his clothes.

We were dressed within minutes. Luke and Rick gave me a ride to where Jake stood in a field with his shirt off, his skin glistening in the hot Texas sun, hammering at a fence post.

"Wonder if Jake will be up for more fun sometime?" Luke wondered out loud.

"He could be," Rick said. "He did enjoy it, that much I know."

"Bye guys, thanks for the lift...and everything," I said as I got out of the truck.

Chapter Twelve

"Hey, Jake!" I called over to him and he looked up with a smile. I could swear his pants got thicker in the front when he saw me. "Glad to see me?" I asked.

"Yeah," He waved at Luke and Rick as they took off in the truck. "I sure am."

"Really?" I said in disbelief.

"Come on. I want to talk to you. Let's go behind those trees over there," he said, pointing the way to a cluster trees. Once we got there, he pulled me close for a hug. "Listen, what we did earlier, I got carried away, but I really…kinda…liked it."

"You're straight, aren't you?"

"Yup," he confirmed. "But I think I might be more flexible than I originally thought. You see, my girl...um...ex girlfriend, well, uh...she used to fuck me sometimes."

"She what?"

"With a dildo. She had this big black dildo she would stick up my ass and fuck me. She was kinky like that. The thing is, I kinda enjoyed it. And sometimes I wondered what it would feel like to have the real thing in there, you know."

"Are you saying you want to be fucked by a man?" I couldn't believe what I was hearing.

"I've been thinking about it ever since we did those things by the pond. It got my juices flowing and my dick hard." He grabbed my hand and placed it on his crotch. "Can you feel how hard it is?" His dick felt as hard as steel. Thick and long. The length went down into his pant leg. Bulging there like a snake.

"Are you asking me to fuck you?" I asked, hesitantly.

"Yeah," he admitted.

"Why not Rick or Luke. You've known them longer. You know they both want you."

"That's the thing. I want it to be with someone who doesn't know me well. I think I would be too embarrassed to ask them. They think of me as this big stud, a lady's man. And despite what happened back there today, I think they still do. Who knows what they will think if they knew I wanted to get fucked."

Hey, I wasn't arguing. I wanted to fuck him. I just wanted to be sure he really wanted it.

"When do you want to do it?"

"Now!' He said enthusiastically.

"I just had an orgasm again with Rick and Luke. I'm not sure I..."

"I can help with that." He squatted down and immediately pulled my jeans and underwear down and took my flaccid dick into his hot mouth, his luscious lips wrapped around my shaft and sucked me in.

"Oh god!" I moaned. For a straight guy, his can suck a mean cock. "How did you get so good at sucking dick?" I asked.

"I practiced with the same dildo my ex used to fuck me. She would sometimes have me put it in my mouth and told me to suck it. I think she really wanted to have a bisexual threesome with another guy but knew I wouldn't go for it." He had pulled off my dick to say that and then went right back at it, sucking my dick back into his hot moist mouth.

"If she could only see you now," I said. "Mmm, oh God!"

My dick became hard almost instantly. Jake's sucking made me horny again. I wanted to fuck his ass soon. I wanted to be the first man, possibly the only man, to go there, to fill him up with my seed.

"We don't have any lube," Jake said, "I'm gonna slick your dick up with my saliva and your pre-cum. It should go in okay since I've been using that dildo."

He got up and removed all his clothes. His giant dick sprang up, a solid black cock with a large mushroom head. I involuntarily licked my lips. It looked so appetizing but was glad it wasn't going up my ass. He turned around for me, showing off his firm ass. Plump, round black orbs of glistening muscles.

"Just eat my ass a little. Make it slick," he said.

I pushed my face into his ass and licked and slobbered all over his hole.

"Ah. Man, that feels good," he said as my tongue poked around his hole. He wiggled his ass and moved back and forth on my tongue. "Yeah! Oh, yeah!"

Soon we were ready to fuck. He leaned against a tree his ass spread open for me. He bent down enough so I was better able to reach his hole. I guided my dick to his opening. It popped through his sphincter. The head was in and it felt amazing.

"Go on," he said, "push it all in. All at once."

I complied. My whole dick, all six hard inches of it, slid into his hole. My bush brushed against his ass cheeks.

"Ah, God!" He moaned. "Wow! It feels so much better than that dildo. Now fuck me, don't be shy. Fuck me hard and fast. I want to feel you cum inside me."

With forceful words like those, how could I resist?

I pulled out and slammed back in, my pelvis hitting his buttocks with a bang. He jacked his long fat prick while I banged his backside repeatedly. Picking up speed and picking up rhythm. His hole had a tight grip on my own much smaller cock. My cock might have only been six inches long, but it was fat and filled his hole.

"Oh Lord! God! Uh!" He shouted as I invaded his hole with my thrusting cock. "Yeah! Fuck me! Oh! Phillip!"

I felt my explosion pending and wanted him to cum with me. I reached around, pushed his hand away, and took over jacking him. His dick felt so heavy in my hand. I slid my hand up and down it as fast as I was fucking him. I was close and sensed he was too.

"Oh God! I'm gonna cum!" I yelled.

"Me too! Oh God! Keep jacking my cock! Ooh!"

Cum shot out of his cock and into the air and over my hand. Jet after jet of thick white liquid splattered all over the place. Jake moaned and thrust his cock through my still jacking hand. At about the same time I shot my load up his insides. Splattering his anal walls. Some leaked out onto my cock as I continued to fuck him.

"Oh God! Yeah! Mmm," I moaned and leaned onto Jake's strong muscular back, which was wet with sweat. His scent intoxicating, a manly odor that permeated my senses.

"Oh God. That was good. I need to do that more often," he said, catching his breath.

"We can talk about that later," I said as I pulled out and smiled at him. "Right now, we better finish up our work or my uncle will have both our hides."

"Yeah," he laughed heartily. "You're right."

When we were done working Jake drove me back to the house. I was exhausted from the work we did and the sex we had. It was almost suppertime and I truly had built up a man-sized appetite.

"Thanks Jake. It was really great working with you."

"I liked working with you too. You worked harder than a lot of guys I know." He studied my face for a moment. "Never kissed a guy before. Do you mind if I lay one on you?"

Shock must have shown on my face. I couldn't believe he had asked me for a kiss.

"Yes. You may kiss me Jake," I gave him permission.

He leaned over and our lips touched. He devoured my mouth, his tongue dueling with mine. We kissed for over a minute. Maybe more. It was hard keeping track of time as it slipped by unnoticed in the throes of passion. He pulled away and smiled shyly.

"Today seems to be a lot of firsts for me," he chuckled.

"Well, better get cleaned for supper," I suggested and we both leaped out of the truck and headed for the house.

Someone grabbed my arm from behind and swung me around, while Jake disappeared inside the house.

It was Rick.

"That seemed cozy," he snarled. "You and Jake kissing like lovers."

"He just wanted to try it out," I informed him, not understanding his jealousy.

"With you?" He growled.

"Did you want to kiss him?" I asked, crossing my arms, thinking he wanted to mess around more with Jake.

"No, I don't want to kiss him. I want to...," he stopped and stared at me, thinking something over. "Oh heck," he grabbed hold of me and pulled me tight and kissed my quivering lips with more passion than I had ever known. The kiss seemed to last forever. He pulled away and I could hardly breathe. "I only want to kiss you," he said and without another word, he walked towards the house.

His tight ass looked hot in his jeans and I wanted to leap myself at him and never let go. I wanted to do with him what Jake and I had done. I wondered if anyone had ever penetrated that ass of his. If he would be open to it like Jake.

My cock throbbed and ached for Rick and my heart was still pounding from that one kiss. I ran up to him. Did he love me the way I have loved him from the beginning? He was at the door when I caught up to him. My breath ragged as I took his hand.

"Rick," I started. "What does the kiss mean?" I wanted to be sure. After what happened with Barry, I needed to be sure.

"It means exactly what you think it means," he said no more and tipped his hat back with a sly smile.

He entered the house and I followed close behind and bumped right smack into him as he stood frozen in place. My heart stopped when I saw who was sitting in the living room with my uncle.

"Rick. Phillip," Uncle Hank said. "Seems we have a visitor. Phillip, I believe you know Barry."

Chapter Thirteen

Barry nervously got up from the couch. He had this preppie look going for him. A sweater vest, tan slacks, and brown suede shoes. He was handsome in a GQ sort of way, with high cheek bones, short auburn hair neatly combed to the side, and he had red rimmed glasses upon his fair face, his pale blue eyes behind them, questioning.

I stood frozen behind Rick, unable to speak. Stunned by the mere presence of this man I once had a crush on but who crushed me so horribly just mere weeks before. Now he was standing in front of me and it was as if time had slipped back.

"Barry," I said, barely audible.

"Phillip," he said coming towards me with his hand extended, as if nothing had happened in our recent past. "Good to see you."

"Who's this?" Rick asked me with concern in his voice.

"Uh...Barry," I told Rick. "Barry Sloane. We were at college together."

"Yeah. But you left and no one seemed to know what happened to you. I was able to contact your parents and asked them where I might find you. I told them it was urgent I see you. Hope you don't mind."

"Urgent?" I asked, still astounded by seeing this man.

"Yeah," he put down his hand, I was so zoned out I didn't even think of shaking it. "I really wanted to see you, to explain things. To apologize for what I did."

"What did you do?" Rick asked, acidly.

"That's none of your business, cowboy," Barry said, snidely.

Rick clenched his fists but said nothing. His eyes shot daggers into Barry.

"Can we talk? Privately?" Barry asked, wary of Rick's intense body language.

"Sure. We can talk outside," I said.

Rick grabbed my arm.

"You sure you want to talk to him?" He asked.

I looked at Barry then back at Rick and nodded.

"I think I better," I told him. "I'll be alright." It warmed my heart that Rick had such concern for me. I knew I needed to talk with Barry, to clear the air and move on with my life, whatever life had in store for me.

When Barry and I were some distance from the house, walking in silence with an uncomfortable air, I finally asked what he wanted to talk about.

"So, what's this all about? You didn't hit me hard enough back in Dallas and thought you'd come to finish me off?"

"I deserve that. Actually, I really did want to apologize. I didn't mean to hit you. It was just a reflex. I've been going nuts trying to find you. Your roommate gave me your parents phone number and I called, told them I was a friend, and they were more than happy to tell me where you had gone."

"There was no need for you to have gone through all that trouble, I got the message."

"No! It's not like that," he insisted. He stopped and reached out for me. "I was scared. When you told me you really liked me...like that, it made me scared. Because I knew I was interested. More then I could have ever admitted. I don't know if I'm gay or bi or just curious, but I did like you. A lot."

He pushed in close to me and touched my lips with his. It was a tentative kiss, void of passion. It reminded me more of a brotherly kiss than one from lovers. Unlike Rick's kiss, his didn't thrill me at all. I pushed him away and shook my head.

"It's too late. I realize what I felt for you was a fleeting flame that flickered and burnt out way too quickly."

"Is it because I punched you in the stomach in front of a crowd of people when you told me you loved me?"

"That didn't help," I admitted. "But there's more. I found someone else."

"That cowboy?" He asked, solemnly.

"Yeah."

"Does he love you?"

"I really don't know. I thought he had a boyfriend, but he has been acting like he wants me and seems to get jealous when I'm with someone else. I would like to find out though."

"Actually, I do understand. I don't like it, but I understand."

"I was hoping you'd be more crushed."

"I only have myself to blame. I pushed you away when I wasn't ready. I didn't expect you to find someone so soon."

"Neither did I."

"If you and that cowboy don't work out, you'll know where to find me."

"Sure," I gave him a weak smile.

The truth of the matter was I wasn't at all sure if Rick really loved me or if there was something else going on with him. I wanted to find out. It was nice to know I could go back to Dallas if it didn't work out. But I didn't want to run away anymore. I liked it here at the ranch. Maybe I could go to a college near by and finish my degree and work on the ranch no matter what happened with Rick and me.

"Kiss goodbye?" Barry asked pleadingly, with puppy dog eyes.

"Of course," We kissed briefly on the lips. I knew with that kiss I would never feel the same about Barry as I once did. He was in my past and the future was wide open. "If you are curious, there are lots of other guys in college who are also curious. Then maybe you can figure things out for yourself," I suggested.

"I wish I never punched you," he said with regret and I laughed a little.

"Me too. But what's done is done. Now go and live your life," I told him.

"Good luck with your cowboy," he kissed me one last time and then walked away to his car and out of my life.

***

"Where's Rick?" I asked Uncle Hank, my breath shaky. I ran all the way back to the house after Barry had left, anxious to have a talk with

Rick.

"He's gone for a ride on his horse. Said he needed to clear is head." Uncle Hank took a long measuring look at me. "Is there something going on between you two?"

"I don't really know, but I gotta find him."

"Maybe Luke might know where he went."

"Sure. Thanks," I said as I went back outside to search for Luke. He was grooming a horse as I approached. "Luke," I said, tentatively, "do you know where Rick might has gone to clear his head. I need to talk with him."

Luke stopped brushing his horse and looked me up and down. His smile was broad, yet his eyes seemed sad.

"You got it bad, don't you?"

"What?"

"You're in love with him, aren't you?"

"I don't really know," I said.

"Sure, you are," he went back to brushing his horse. "Who wouldn't be? I was in love with him once myself."

"Are you still? In love with him, I mean?"

"We'll always be best buds, but we've both moved on. I get the feeling he's hung up on you."

"Really?" I said. "I can't believe someone like him would go for someone like me."

"Tastes can vary. And you're very cute, in case you didn't know it. I think I know where we might find him. I'll take you there. Just let me saddle up my horse and we'll be on our way."

"Wait. Can't we go by truck?"

"Why go by truck when we have a horse?"

That made sense, I think.

A few moments later Luke and his horse, Rainbow, a beautiful black stallion, came trotting up next to me. High on his horse Luke seemed bigger than life. With his white cowboy hat and his golden locks gleaming in the fading sun.

"Come on," he said, reaching for my hand. He pulled me up and I swung my legs around the saddle. "Okay, now hang on but no funny business."

I wrapped my arms around his waist as we galloped away.

***

"I think he's probably in there," he said pointing to a rustic old shack. "See, there's his horse. He likes to come here and think. He calls it his thinking shack."

"Oh," I said. Something about it reminded me of the 'love shack' back at the house.

"Look, Phillip," He said as I got down from his horse. "I thought about renewing our relationship, such as it was. But I could tell he was hooked on you."

"Really? I didn't know he was. I thought he was back with you."

"No, He made that clear the first day I was back. He wasn't into it when we started to fool around. And so, we didn't do anything. Not until that time at the pond with you and Jake. He got real excited when you got naked. I could tell. He couldn't keep his eyes off you. Hell, I wanted a piece of you myself. I know that Rick has real feelings for you though. Even though he might not have said it yet."

"But we've only just met less than a week ago."

"You feel the same about him, don't you? Love at first sight, I guess. Soul mates that are meant to be. Something has a pull on you both, like magnets."

I petted Rainbow's forehead as I pondered what Luke had said.

"I best be leaving you two alone," Luke said. "I got a feeling the thinking shack might turn into the love shack." he grinned. "If you're late for supper, I think we'll understand." He winked and then he rode off back to the house.

Taking a deep breath, I walked to the entrance of the shack and opened it. It was dusty and dark. A gas lantern was the only light. Rick stretched out on a cot with a thin and lumpy mattress. He glanced up as I walked in.

"That looks uncomfortable," I said as I sat down on an upturned bucket.

100

"It is. But I'm used to it," he fiddled with his thumbs. "So...um...are you going to be leaving us?"

"No. Why?"

"Oh. I thought he came back to take you back to Dallas. I saw you two kissing."

"That was a goodbye kiss. He just came by to apologize for the way he treated me." I sat there a moment studying him. Wondering if he truly loved me or if this was all leading up to one colossal let down. "He wanted to maybe try stuff with me, but I told him I was no longer interested."

"Why not? From what I could see he's nice looking. And that's what you wanted, wasn't it?"

"He's not the one I want."

"Oh," he said looking back at me, questioning. "And who do you want?"

"Okay. I'm gonna put it all on the line here," another deep breath, "if you don't want me then I'll still stay here and we can be friends, I'm not going to run away like I did with Barry, but I loved you from the first moment I saw you."

He sprang up from the cot and grabbed me, holding me tight.

"I want you too," he whispered in my ear. "I think I loved you since that first day. When I saw you with Diego and Brad, I was so jealous. I wanted to hate you but couldn't. I had no right to be possessive of you."

"I thought you were back together with Luke. When I saw you two together my heart sank."

"No. We're friends, but I don't think I could love him the same as I do you."

Rick pulled me into a passionate kiss. His tongue fought and won entrance into my mouth and found my own tongue. Our tongues clashed together and fought a duel as our lips were smashed in a collaboration of fervent arousal. He tore open my shirt, buttons flying everywhere. He yanked the shirt off me and kissed down my chest finding my nipples. He sucked them and teased them, sending torrents of pleasure through my body. His big cowboy hand groped my crotch and squeezed my hard dick through my jeans. He undid my belt and jeans and slid them down along with my underwear. My dick was swollen and leaking. He knelt and licked the head, then took my jeans and underwear off completely as well as my shoes and socks. He guided me to the cot and had me to lie down on it.

My legs were spread wide as he massaged my thighs and fondled my balls. He went down on my cock in one swift swoop, swallowing it all, bobbing his head fast upon it, his tongue swirling around the shaft as he sucked. My body was afire, and my head felt like it might explode. The sensations he gave me was like no other.

He got up off my dick and tore his clothes off as fast he could. His naked body stood before me. His cock magnificently commanded attention. I reached up and grabbed it, licking around the head. He shuddered with ecstasy.

"I want you to fuck me," he said, breathlessly.

I gazed into his lust filled dark eyes.

"What?" I couldn't believe what he was asking me to do.

"Fuck me. Please."

"Have you ever been..."

"No. But I want to. I want you to be the first and only guy to fuck me."

He knelt on the floor and got something from under the cot. It was a bottle of lube.

"I keep this here in case I bring someone here to fuck."

He squeezed some onto his hand and smeared it on my dick.

"Oh God," his jacking hand felt good on my dick. "I thought the love shack was behind the house," I said, as his hand slid up and down my shaft.

"This is more private. I hardly ever used the shack behind the house. Don't worry, you're the only one allowed here now," he smiled. "Put some on my hole," he said.

He leaned forward over the cot and spread his ass cheeks for me. It was a beautiful sight. His perfectly round and tanned ass cheeks with his hole between them, awaiting my attention. I got down on my knees and squirted some lube onto my fingers and rubbed them into his hole. I wiggled them and opened his hole as best I could.

"Oh God, yes. You have such a tender touch." He gasped.

He whimpered and moaned as my fingers dug deeper. I added more lube and continued to dig. My free hand wrapped around his cock and jerked him, slowly. I licked his low hanging balls and sucked on them.

"Oh God! I want you to fuck me now!" He screamed. "I need your dick inside me," he begged.

Aiming my dick, I pushed the head inside his tight hole.

"Oh God!" He moaned. "It takes some getting used to, doesn't it?"

"You want me to pull out?" I asked.

"No!" He demanded. "Don't you dare! Go on. Put more in."

I pushed in another couple of inches. He sighed and moaned but didn't complain.

"I love you, Rick," I said, kissing his back.

"I love you too, Phillip."

My cock slid in the rest of the way, now buried deep inside him.

"Oh God!" He shouted. "Fuck me, Phillip. Fuck me now!"

I moved my hips back and forth. Pulling out and slamming back in, his hole had a tight grip on my cock. The velvety warmth of his hole on my sensitive cock made me quiver with ecstasy. Seeing his broad back, his ass cheeks spread open, my cock going in and out of his hole, sent shivers throughout my whole being. I was fucking Rick and he was loving it, moaning, and gasping, and begging for more.

I banged him hard, his balls were dancing between his thick muscled legs, his dick stiff and leaking pre-cum onto the grimy floor below.

I pulled out and had him turn around and scoot up on the cot against the wall. His legs were sticking straight into the air and he held them up as I plunged back into his tight hole. I fucked him hard and fast. He screamed with pleasure as I plowed him. I bent over to lick his sweaty chest. He grabbed my head and mashed it down onto his dewy skin. I licked and kissed, then he guided my face to his and our lips touched once more in a fiery kiss.

I pulled out of him once more and helped him up. We stood in an embrace and kissed. Our dicks smashed against one another.

Suddenly, he broke our kiss and pushed me back onto the cot. He pulled the cot out from the wall, with me writhing on it, my cock standing tall. He straddled the cot and guided my cock back into his hole. He rose and slid back down on my dick; riding it like the cowboy he always will be. He bounced on my cock for several minutes. Fucking himself on my hard pole. I saw it going in and out of his hole as his dick bounced and danced around, slapping my stomach.

As I felt my orgasm approach, I reached out and grabbed his cock, sliding my hand up and down it. Jacking him as he continued to fuck himself on my cock. "Oh God!" He yelled. "Gonna cum! Gonna fucking cum!" Sperm spat out of his cock and down on my jacking hand. "Ah! Yeah!" Shot after shot of white thick creamy cum exploded from his cock.

His hole had a tight grip on my own cock and my own orgasm was fast approaching.

"Oh God! Oh God!" I shouted. My cock erupted within Rick's bowels, load after load. Some leaked from his hole as I kept shooting. "Ooh! God!"

He bent down to resume our kissing. My softening cock slipped out of his used hole. He laid out on top of me, kissing me and holding me.

Once we recovered from our orgasms, we got dressed and got on his horse for the ride back to the house.

"You think we're late for supper?" I asked.

"Maybe by an hour or so. See, it's already dark."

"Think they missed us?"

"Just hope there are some leftovers. Sex can build up a man's appetite."

"If you don't mind," Rick said, "the bunk house can get pretty crowded and rowdy sometimes. Mind if I bunk with you tonight?" He asked.

My smile widened behind him as we rode his horse home.

"I was hoping you'd ask. You can bunk with me anytime. But do you think we'll get much sleep?"

"Not likely. But who cares."

I didn't. That's for sure.

When we made it back to the house, Uncle Hank was on the porch with Clem. He looked at the two of us funny.

"You boys hungry?" He asked.

"Starving," Rick said, with a side glance to me.

"Rosa's keeping your food warm. What happened to your shirt, Phillip?" Uncle Hank asked.

I had forgotten about the buttons.

"Well...um..."

"Just something that happened in the heat of passion," Rick jumped in.

"Oh...I see...well...yes," My uncle stuttered. "Come on Clem, time for our bath."

Chapter Fourteen

Everyone wanted to go to Christmas Eve services, leaving Rick and me alone in the house. We decided not to go so we can have some alone time. Everyone understood. We sat on a sofa, cuddling together by the fireplace, with the Christmas tree twinkling multicolored lights as the stereo played Christmas music. I never felt more content in my life.

My eyes were getting heavy when Rick kissed me on top of my head.

"You want to do it?" He whispered in my ear, making me fully alert. I knew what he meant by *'do it.'*

"My room or yours?" I was definitely up for it. We had done it several times since that day in the shack a week before, and I never could get enough.

"How about here?" Rick suggested.

"In the living room?"

"Sure, I think it's a romantic setting with the fireplace and Christmas lights, and music playing."

I smiled warmly at him. Rick, my darling, loving boyfriend, can be very romantic.

"Okay," I pulled my shirt off. "Anything you want."

"Anything?" He caressed his chin with his fingers and thought for a moment. "I want you to fuck me over that couch but first, let's get in a sixty-nine."

I didn't hesitate, and once we shed our clothes, we laid out by the fire in the sixty-nine position. My hardening cock went right into his mouth while I took his in mine. I loved running my hands over his thighs while I sucked him, and over his hairy pubic region. And I loved feeling his strong rough hand caressing my soft, nearly hairless skin.

I licked down his long shaft and found his juicy balls, slobbering on them and sucking them into my mouth. He mirrored my movements. I sucked on his balls for a while and moved my hand behind him to find his no longer virgin hole. He moved back up to my cock as I finger fucked him while I stayed attached to his balls for a little longer. After a few minutes, I moved back to his leaking cock head and licked and sucked my way down to his base. I made progress over the last couple of times sucking him in devouring his whole cock into my mouth. I reached his pubic area without much of a problem.

"Oh, God yeah!" He shouted. He loved it when I deep throated him.

When he did the same to me, I yelped, and dug deeper into his hole. I loved it too.

"Oh God, I'm ready for you to fuck me," he said, taking his mouth off my cock.

He spread himself over the plaid couch, spreading his legs a bit, his beautiful plump ass facing me. My dick twitched in anticipation.

I loved fucking my sweet lover.

After lubing up I got up behind him on the couch, found his tight hole, and stuck my dripping cock inside, slowly pushing in. He grunted and wiggled as my cock slid inside the soft velvety walls of his ass.

"Oh, Phillip. I love your dick in me. I love you so much," he said.

I kissed him softly on the neck.

"I love you too, Rick. You're the best thing that's ever happened to me."

"You're the best thing that's ever happened to me too," he turned his head back and we kissed on the lips for a minute.

He turned back and braced his hands on the couch. I plunged in and out of his manly ass. Shivers went up my spine as I entered him again and again. When I looked down to see my cock appearing and disappearing between his two golden globes of flesh, I about lost it, it was an erotic tantalizing sight.

"I'm going to cum!" I yelled out as I felt my balls boiling over with the sweet juices of my loins.

"Cum!" He yelled back. "Cum in my ass, lover."

"Ah, I... God!" I held on for dear life, my arms around his muscular chest as I released my load in my lover's ass.

"Ah...uh...wow." I collapsed on his back, resting my head there, recovering from the intense feeling Rick gave to me, the juices of my seed deep in his ass.

"Don't pull out yet," he warned.

He slowly pushed himself from the couch while I held onto his sturdy mid-section. He walked us over by the fireplace with my cock still lodged deep in his perky ass.

"Okay," he said. I pulled out and cum dribbled down his backside. "Didn't want to get the couch messy and sticky with cum."

He got on his knees and licked me clean and then he laid on the floor and I did the same to him. I took his cock in my mouth and bobbed up and down until he had an explosion of his own.

With both of us spent, we cuddled the rest of the evening by the fire. I knew we would make love again later that night.

We were roasting marshmallows when the front door flew open and everyone clambered inside, singing and being joyful.

"Hey," Erika greeted us with a bright smile. What did you two do tonight?"

"Erika," Uncle Hank said. "I don't think it's any of our business."

"Ah, Hank," Rick said, pulling out his marshmallow from the flames. "We just roasted marshmallows." He took a bite of the blackened, gooey sweet.

"Yup. Sure," Luke shook his head. "That's all you did. We believe that like we believe reindeer can fly."

"Of course, they can fly," I countered. "What are you trying to tell me Luke?" Everyone laughed, including Luke.

***

On Christmas morning, we all rose and rushed downstairs. However, Rick and I had to take care of morning wood first with a quick sixty-nine session.

Rosa had a big breakfast ready for us at the table.

"Sorry Rosa, Phillip and I just ate," Rick joked, and I flashed him a look. Erika couldn't help but giggle. Rosa looked confused. Uncle Hank cleared his throat. Luke covered his ears. Jake shook his head. Diego

108

and Brad shrugged. Todd snickered. And Clem scratched his head.

After breakfast, we all went into the living room for gift opening time. I was kind of excited but wasn't expecting much. I managed to buy everyone a gift with the little bit of money I had stashed away.

We exchanged gifts and tore the fancy wrapping paper open. Everyone seemed to love everything they got. I got some much-needed new clothes, and cowboy boots that Luke had gotten me fit perfectly. Don't know how he knew my size. I also got a new cowboy hat.

"Hey, now you're beginning to look like a real cowboy," Rick said. "Maybe this will make you feel even more like one," he handed me a small box.

There was a picture of Blaze inside a gold frame.

"A picture of your horse," I said, amazed. She looked beautiful in the photo.

"No," Rick said. "A picture of your horse."

I looked up at him, too stunned for words. Tears ran down my face. I couldn't believe he would give me his horse.

"But.," what I started to say, I really didn't know.

"I know how much you like her," he said. "Erika told me how you admired her that day you two went riding and I wanted to give you the perfect gift, a little piece of my heart. I have another horse, old Lightning."

"Lightning, huh?" I remembered when Erika and I talked about names for horses.

"Yup. So, we can go riding together every day. Though, I kinda liked it when you rode on the back of the horse with me."

"We can still do that sometimes."

"I suppose we could," he kissed the top of my head with everyone looking at us. My face was a beet red. "Gosh, I never seen anyone blush as much as you." Then he kissed my lips briefly. "You want to go for a ride before lunch?"

"Sure do," I said, ready to spend some alone time with Rick.

"Not just yet, you two," Uncle Hank halted us. "I got one more thing for Phillip." He handed me an unopened package.

"Really?" I said, taking it.

"It's actually something Clem and I got you. I think you'll enjoy it immensely."

I tore open the package and found some papers inside. They looked official.

The deed to the Ranch!

"What the...," I stood there, stunned.

"Me and Clem have decided to retire and move to Hawaii. Clem always wanted to live there, but not for another two years so we can stick around and show you the ropes of ranching. You can still go back to college if you like and learn all you can there. But this ranch is now yours. It's official."

"But why...I mean, why me?"

"Well, I never did have a son and neither did Clem, you're the closest thing we ever had."

I was touched and new tears appeared, rolling down my face.

"I love it uncle," I hugged him. "It's the best present, besides my horse, that I have ever gotten."

"How about them boots?" Luke said. "You gotta love them boots."

"I do. I love everything I got today, most of all, all of you, my new family. And especially you," I looked lovingly at Rick. "You are my heart and soul."

"Now, how 'bout that ride?" Rick asked.

"You bet," I rushed into his strong arms and he held me tight.

I noticed Erika had tears in her eyes as she gazed upon the scene.

"Christmas always make me cry," she sniffled.

***

As Christmas drifted away and the New Year fast approaching, I knew I would never be parted from Rick. Of that I was sure. Our love will last as long as Uncle Hank's and Clem's, even longer. For as long as the world spins.

The New Year will see me start at a nearby college and learning the ropes from Uncle Hank and Clem. Rick and I had decided his place was with me, so he moved from the bunkhouse into my room. I was starting a new chapter in my life, one that will always include Rick, along with the other friends I've made.

Going into town one day, Uncle Hank and Clem were in the front of the truck while Luke, Rick and I were in the back. We stopped at the gas station across from the diner. We got out from the back and saw Sam coming over to us. He was excited to see us again.

"Hi Rick, Phillip" he greeted us. Sam had found out about us one day when we were eating out and Sam came over to our table. He seemed a bit jealous but accepted the fact Rick was now my boyfriend.

Luke gave an appraising look to Sam.

"What, no hello to me, Sam," Luke said.

"Uh...sure, sorry. Hello." Sam smiled at the handsome cowboy.

"Do you mind showing me the way to the restroom, Sam? Been a while since I been here," Luke said.

"Sure," Sam smiled broadly. "This way."

Luke followed Sam towards the back of the gas station. Luke looked back and winked at us.

"Love blooming you think?" Rick asked.

"Ain't no telling," I said.

Rick let out a big whoop.

"I knew I would rub off on you," he held me tight and kiss me tenderly.

"And that ain't no lie," I smiled up at my handsome boyfriend.

As we rode off into the sunset, cuddled in the back of the pick-up, I knew my life was going to be an amazing adventure with my cowboy by my side.

The End

www.ingramcontent.com/pod-product-compliance
Lightning Source LLC
Chambersburg PA
CBHW072102150726
47999CB00005B/1849